Babbling
Brooks

Babbling Brooks

Sequel to Jars of Nails

A novel by
Gabriel Godard

iUniverse, Inc.
New York   Bloomington

iUniverse books may be ordered through booksellers or by contacting:

*iUniverse
1663 Liberty Drive
Bloomington, IN 47403
www.iuniverse.com
1-800-Authors (1-800-288-4677)*

*ISBN: 978-1-4401-3043-4 (sc)
ISBN: 978-1-4401-3044-1 (ebook)*

Printed in the United States of America

iUniverse rev. date: 03/26/09

This book is dedicated to my family, friends and students. You've made my dreams come true. You know who you are, and I thank you.

To my beautiful wife Gaye, you are my life.

Special thanks goes to Melanie, Jordan, Erin, Kathi, Jerry, Becky and Emily for their help.

This book is in memory of William Russell Sr. and Ronnie Hill. You will not be forgotten.

CHAPTER 1

JEFF BROOKS RESTED inside his 1993 white van filled with thousands in cash stashed in a floorboard safe. He and the late Cory Blake had sweated for hours as they designed and built the hidden safe. In the distance blinding yellow sunshine ripple off the ocean. Obscuring the horizon a translucent figure approaches along the beach. Sophia Martinez' wore a silky beige dress that revealed her hourglass figure and firm breasts. Her long dark hair danced in the wind as sunlight passed through its long strands. Jeff's heart fluttered as he watched what must have been a mirage.

A tall blonde man wearing blue jeans, a navy blue T-shirt and a black baseball cap greeted Sophia. The bleach blonde hair clashed with the ball cap, much like white socks with black shoes. She stopped to speak to the handsome stranger, which made Jeff churn with jealousy. The conversation seemed to grow in intimacy quickly as Sophia threw her hair back and lightly brushed the stranger's arm. Jeff scrambled to get dressed and began to panic as he searched for his clothing.

Finally dressed, Jeff reached for the door handle but found it missing. The tall stranger lovingly brushed

Sophia's hair from her shoulder. Jeff looked for a way out, but all the door handles were missing and the windows tightly shut. When Sophia and the stranger approached the vehicle holding hands, Jeff had a flash of recognition. Spittle flew from Jeff's mouth as he roared in fear, "You bastard get away from her! Haven't you done enough? Sophia, run!" Jeff kicked the windshield, bracing himself against the driver's seat to get maximum force. The window seemed to laugh at his feeble attempt to break free.

Heat rose from the sand as they stopped and embraced. "Why is this happening to me?" Jeff wondered. The stranger pulled out a long surgical knife from the rear of his pants and pulled back Sophia's head exposing her neck. He pecked tenderly as he kissed the softness of her neck. At the sight of the knife, Jeff threw everything he could find in the van as he tried desperately to smash through the glass.

The stranger stopped embracing her neck and looked toward Jeff with a wink and a crooked grin. In one smooth motion he sliced through the vulnerable victim's neck, showering the van's windshield with blood. Jeff thrashed inside the van in disbelief from what his eyes had just witnessed. When Sophia's body stopped pumping out blood, the stranger released her hair, allowing her to plummet toward the ground making a hollow thud as she hit.

Jeff felt as drained as his beloved Sophia. The stranger approached the van and stood next to the driver's side door with his head tilted down. The ball cap covered his face. Slowly, Cory Blake lifted his head to reveal his face to Jeff.

Cory spoke in a slow deliberate tone. "Jeff, why are you so upset? I did this for us. You are nothing without me. I am nothing without you. Come with me, Jeff. Why are you screaming? Don't you understand me?"

Jeff stared at the dead man from his past. He screamed in terror as he watched Cory raise his hand with the super glued Smith & Wesson .38 to his temple and pull the trigger. The skull flexed like a pumpkin under great pressure as the bullet passed through. A red mist shot out from the blast. He remained on his feet, staring into Jeff's eyes while a slow steady stream of blood poured from the hole.

Jeff Brooks babbled incoherently as his diaphragm filled with air to work itself into a terror scream. Sophia shook him hard to release him from his nightmare. Sophia kept repeating, "Jeff, you are safe. Jeff, you are safe." The windows and walls inside the van dripped with condensation as the ocean lapped a steady rhythm on the beach.

After ten minutes of silence, Sophia finally asked, "Jeff, what was your nightmare about?"

"Just an unwelcome visit from a past demon." As Jeff guardedly answered in a croaky voice he felt as if an angry spirit invaded his body.

CHAPTER 2

OR THE LAST three weeks, Jeff had lived in his van
parked on the edge of Sophia's father's farm. He had
come to know the Martinez family as God-fearing
Mexicans who held family traditions close to their hearts.
On this morning, the sun blazed through the makeshift
yellow curtain used to divide the seats and the cargo area
of the van where Jeff slept. He watched the side of Sophia's
chest rise and lower with each breath as she slept soundly,
snuggled to his right side. He wondered if restful sleep
would ever come to him again. Sleep had become his
enemy ever since that fateful day when he left Cory on a
bench outside of Geary Hospital with a severed spine and
a gun glued to his palm.

After running away from Junction City, Jeff finally
stopped in Zempoala, Mexico, a small coastal farming
town nestled near the slopes of the Sierra Madre Oriental
mountain chain. The chain parallels the Gulf Coast in
central Mexico. The term, "breathtaking" really did not
do it justice. "Heaven on earth" was probably closer to
the truth.

As Sophia began to come out of her sleep, she did
a morning stretch against his body with a tiny shiver

and a purr. She rolled on top of her mighty American lover and caressed his smooth, well-defined chest. Even without sleep Jeff's body would always respond to a wake up call of this nature. As their rhythm and speed increased, they both reached paradise together. After the explosion in Jeff's mind from the orgasm, he thought that this physical connection surpassed any psychiatric session money could buy. Yet still, uninterrupted sleep eluded him.

For the last several days, Sophia had been leaving her room at night, once her parents were asleep, to meet Jeff by the fire pit on the beach. In the morning, she would feed the chickens before re-entering the farmhouse. The plan seemed to be flawless. If her parents asked, she was up early feeding the chickens. That morning, when Jeff showed up at the farmhouse an hour after Sophia for breakfast, everyone looked upset.

Alfonso Martinez looked up at Jeff as he entered the farmhouse kitchen area and motioned him back out the door. Jeff followed Al into the chicken coop. Al turned and began speaking in very rapid Spanish. "You may be here on my land with permission. You provide us with an income by paying for your meals, but milk is not free. I will not let you break my daughter's heart. The milk is not free."

Jeff's Spanish was average at best and he understood enough of this conversation to know that he had upset the Martinez family. This was the last thing he wanted to do. When they had discovered Sophia missing in the middle of the night, all signs pointed to Jeff on the beach.

He replied in his best Spanish, "Señor Martinez, I

love your daughter Sophia. She is the most important person in my life. I promise to never hurt her."

Al grabbed a chicken from a separate caged pen and pointed the hatchet at Jeff. He brought down the hatchet across the chicken's neck and the head popped off. He grabbed the headless, gyrating chicken by the feet and tied it to the fence to drain. With blood dripping from the hatchet, Al pointed his index finger at Jeff and added in broken English, "You'd better not hurt her!"

CHAPTER 3

THINGS IMPROVED DRAMATICALLY with the Martinez family over the next several months. Jeff became less of a stranger and more of a family member. Sophia floated with joy. Her family's acceptance made her feel as if the puzzle pieces of her life were falling into place. The bond between Al and Jeff grew with each day. Jeff radiated when his new father figure offered him praise. For the second time in twenty-six years of life, Jeff took a leap of faith and spoke to Al next to the pigpen. Al stopped serving the slop as Jeff approached.

Jeff looked nervous and in his best Spanish said, "Señor Martinez, as you know, I love Sophia with all my heart and very much wish to make her my wife. I am asking you for your blessing." He held his breath.

Al knew that to stand in the way of the inevitable would be a mistake. Sophia, his oldest child, was now twenty-one. She had never been happier. Al's smile broadened. He opened his arms and the two men embraced.

"Welcome to the family. May you have love forever in your heart and the joy of tiny feet in your house! Come, we must tell everyone the good news. This afternoon the twins and I must make a delivery, but tomorrow I will take you boar hunting for a huge feast on the beach." As he spoke, Al intently stared at his future son-in-law. The twins were Sophia's nineteen-year-old brothers Garcia and Jesus. Jeff could not yet tell them apart.

"Señor Martinez, please wait until I speak to Sophia before sharing the good news. She and I will be taking our walk on the beach this morning." Jeff showed Al the engagement rings he would be presenting Sophia. They were his mother's rings that he had brought with him from Junction City.

At that moment, Sophia exited her parents' home with a bounce in her step, dressed in a lovely purple sundress with yellow flowers. She radiated. They took off and walked hand in hand along the beach, enjoying the sunshine on their skin.

The entire Martinez clan came out to observe the miracle of love unfold from the porch. Jeff made sure to keep Sophia's back to the farmhouse. When they were about four hundred yards away. Jeff thought he could hear Sophia's mother sob in the distance as he dropped down to one knee.

Jeff pulled out the ring box and opened it for Sophia to see. "Sophia, you are the love of my life. I want to grow old with you, build a beautiful house of stone on your father's land and have so many children we will lose count of them." Sophia squealed with joy and shouted, "Yes! Yes, Jeff!"

Overjoyed with the results, Jeff kissed Sophia then picked her up over his shoulder and ran straight into the cold ocean. She laughed and shouted with glee. The couple returned to the farmhouse, dripping wet as the Martinez family applauded their approval.

CHAPTER 4

THE TAN COLOURED Toyota pickup truck seemed to defy gravity as it worked its way over rough terrain. Jeff soaked up the experience with great delight. For the first time in his life he was experiencing a true father-son moment. Jeff's real father had left him at a young age and, although his mother had dated often, there were never any real father figures in his life. The truck teetered on three wheels as it climbed over boulders. The dogs in the back of the pickup barked with excitement as they jostled in their crates.

After a few hours of searching the hills, Al tapped Jeff's left hand and pointed to a wild boar six hundred yards away on the other side of a ravine. "There is our prize, Jeff." Jeff could barely see the animal in the dense brush. Al passed him the binoculars so he could get a better look. Jeff had never seen anything like it. The beast's beige fur looked coarse, with black and brown patches. It had the shape of a large pig and two large tusks protruded from its snout.

Jeff wore a burlap poncho style coat and hand made leather overalls that were lent to him by one of the twins, although he wasn't sure which one. The weapon he was given to bring down the ferocious beast was a knife with a six-inch blade. Al could see the worried look on Jeff's face and added, "Don't worry, gringo, the dogs will do all the work."

Jeff spoke to Al. "Do you normally bring Garcia and Jesus on your hunting trips?"

Al laughed. "Jesus, yes. But Garcia, no. The dogs and Garcia don't get along. They say that dogs can smell fear. I am not sure if that is what brings them such a dislike. But whenever I would bring the boys along for a hunt Garcia never enjoyed it. He is happier on the farm with animals that don't fight back." Jeff swallowed hard at the last statement.

"Señor Martinez, I notice that you have a pistol. This seems unconventional for boar hunting."

"Don't worry Jeff. The pistol is only if things get out of hand. Let's go."

Al unlocked the gate to release the three dogs from the pickup's dog crates. They scrambled out of the crates in a great flurry. Al gave out a high-pitched hiss and the dogs sat in a row at attention. Al motioned for Jeff to start walking and the two men led the way with the dogs in tow. Jeff could barely keep up with Al, who was surely twenty years older. As they climbed up the side of the ravine, Jeff grabbed a branch to hoist himself up onto a rock and he felt searing pain in his hand. He let out a groan and Al responded, "Ah, Nolina. You Gringos know it as bear brush. I forgot to tell you. The plant looks harmless enough, but if you turn over the leaf you will notice the thorns. The poison on the leaf is mild. That scratch will burn for ten minutes or so."

Jeff began to wonder what he had gotten himself into. The dogs still lagged behind in their own little world. They approached the area where they had spotted the boar earlier. The rough terrain they traveled made Jeff feel like they had been hunting for days.

Al spoke quietly, "We will go up this incline to the next ridge so that we can come down on top of the pig." Jeff simply nodded with exhaustion. He couldn't let Al make him look like a retired jock.

Jeff began to climb, making sure to avoid the bear brush. When he reached for a handful of grass to pull himself up, he yelped in pain again. This time Al gave a chuckle and simply stated, "Spear grass. The name needs no explanation." Hidden inside the grass were very sharp plant spikes. Jeff's palm had a pattern of tiny pinpricks of blood. Al chuckled and said, "Good news, no poison." Jeff began to doubt that this male bonding moment was worth his agony.

Jeff caught up with Al who sat on a rock resting with his dogs. The dogs had overtaken Jeff about a kilometer back. Clearly they were used to Al's pace. He smiled at Jeff. "You okay?"

Jeff smiled back and he lied. "Yes, couldn't be better."

Al commanded the dogs. "Get the pig. Get the pig!"

Jeff stood amazed as he watched the dogs go to work immediately, noses to the ground in a soundless search. Finally, the black lab dog caught the scent and the others followed.

Al explained, "The other two dogs are basically putting on a show until that black one picks up the scent. He is the only one with a good nose." The dogs took off through the brush and the men followed close behind. In the distance they heard a splash followed by a lot of primal grunting and snorting from the boar as all three dogs began to bark.

CHAPTER 5

J EFF'S YOUTH AND size didn't seem to give him any advantage as Al took off down the hill like a sure-footed billy goat. In Jeff's attempt to catch up, he lost his footing, slid down the embankment past Al, and dropped into the ravine with a splash. He found himself smack dab in the middle of a fight for survival. The distraction worked to the boar's advantage as it tossed the black and white spotted dog into the air with its tusks. The dog gave a tormented almost humanlike yell before it splashed into the water. Up close, the boar was nothing short of a monster weighing twice as much as the large lab. The boar turned toward its new attacker and Jeff scrambled for his knife. Jeff thanked God for his wet trousers because he was fairly sure he had just pissed his pants. Just as the boar closed in on him, the veteran black lab bit into its right hindquarter and held on as the boar began circling. The brown ridgeback dog took its cue and latched onto the other side of the boar's belly. The boar turned and poked the ridgeback with its tusk.

Al looked like a man possessed as he assessed the situation. Having seen enough damage to his dogs, Al removed his knife from its sheath. Even though the ridgeback was injured, it went after the boar again, this time latching onto the other hindquarter. The black lab never relinquished its hold, its strong jaws clamped onto the rear of the boar. The boar now turned toward Jeff and fixed him as its new target. Al used this distraction to take action. He took two long strides toward the boar and plunged his knife into the side of the beast. Al gave a twist and a wiggle of the knife and stepped away. Like a home-run hitter in baseball, Al didn't wait to see the ball go over the fence. The boar dropped dead as Al picked up the black and white dog, cupped his hand around its muzzle and gave three quick breaths. He repeated this procedure until the dog gave out two sharp coughs.

"Jeff, take off your shoelace and cut it in half. Bring it here and hold the dog by its head." Al commanded Jeff and Jeff did as he was told. The violence he'd just witnessed brought back a flood of emotion from his own past and he welcomed a menial task to distract him. He fought the waves of nausea that seemed to bring the taste of acidic bile from his stomach to his tongue.

Jeff observed the damage done to the black and white dog for the first time. The dog's intestines protruded from a five-inch gash to its side. Al worked quickly as Jeff held the struggling dog. He poked holes with his knife on both sides of the wound and passed the shoelace back and forth creating a suture. As he did this, he very carefully pushed the dog's intestines back into place.

Al finished up and added, "That is going to leave a mark, I'm afraid. It's in God's hands now. Jeff, you hold him while I finish the pig. " Al said as he finished up.

Al grabbed the boar by its front leg and the animal's body twitched from spontaneous nerve firings. The amount of blood in the ravine increased ten fold as he eviscerated the animal, spilling its insides into the ravine. He then pulled the heart from the boar and threw it to the black lab that caught it like a tennis ball and ate it.

He commanded Jeff. "Jeff, we must get Lucky home quickly if she is to live. I know you have never done this before, but I need you to backpack the pig to the truck. I may need to breathe life into Lucky again." Jeff just nodded. He felt guilty about falling into the ravine in the first place. So with Al's help the boar was hoisted onto Jeff's back, the front hooves went over his shoulders and were tied together. The walk back to the truck left Jeff numb in every way. He felt blood and water trickle down his back and into his pants as he walked with the boar on his back. The boar's head rocked back and forth with every step, seemingly in agreement with Jeff's thoughts. Jeff panted from the extra weight on his back. This situation made him flashback to carrying Cory Blake's unconscious body to the van. Yes, the boar nodded in agreement.

Cory will surely come to visit Jeff while he sleeps.

CHAPTER 6

SOPHIA AND MARIA greeted their men as the vehicle stopped. Upon their return from the war with the boar they were treated like heroes. The afternoon's trauma seemed to melt away with Sophia's embrace and the heat of the evening. Al and Jeff carried the boar over to the old, gray wooden barn, where Al quickly went to work showing him how to properly hang the boar to let the meat age for flavor and tenderness. He stuck his nose inside the rib cage and sniffed.

"Jeff, take a smell inside the pig." Jeff did as he requested and the boar smelled like a pack of bacon when it is first opened, only with a slightly gamey-odour. Al continued, "Sometimes you will open up an animal and you can smell that it was sick or unhealthy. Sort of a sour smell."

Jeff asked, "What do you do with the animal in that case?"

"I'll keep the head and hooves for the dogs. It keeps them hungry for the next pig and the rest will go to the offal pit." Al liked this inquisitive young man.

"What's an awful pit? You mean like where awful things go?" Jeff wondered about the name of the pit.

"No. It is an offal pit. See over there, past the chicken and pig barn, where the grass is always green? That is where the soil has become rich from the carcasses of animals that were not fit to eat. It is deep and covered with a heavy lid. Let's go wash up and check on Lucky." Al gave a hearty laugh and shook his head.

As Jeff washed off the blood from his hands and arms with the garden hose, Sophia snuck up behind him and tickled his love handles (even though he didn't have any).

Jeff. "Hey there, beautiful. How is my Mexican goddess this afternoon?"

She gave a large pout and laughed. "I am much better now that you are back and safe. How was hunting with my father? Are you a murderer now?" That last question hit a nerve and he realized that she knew nothing of the bank heist or of Cory.

He stared into her beautiful comical face. It was Jeff's turn to laugh. "I was more of a witness than an active player." He told her the whole story including having trouble keeping up with her father, sliding past him on the slope, landing next to the pig, the Nolina, the spear grass and carrying the pig back.

"He probably won't be able to move tomorrow from trying to show you up. Sounds like you had fun. At least you survived." Sophia laughed.

Jeff remembered Lucky. "Speaking of surviving, Lucky was hurt really bad. Where would your dad have put her while she heals?"

They walked over to the front porch with the view of the ocean. There, on her side, was Lucky sleeping on a burlap sack in a cardboard box. Sophia tenderly stroked the dog's head. "Poor thing." Just then Al appeared beside them. Jeff was startled by how quietly Al could move.

"This is as good a time as any to tell you how happy I am for you both and that I give you my blessing." All three of them embraced. Al nodded toward Lucky. "It will be touch and go for her all night. We will know by morning whether or not she'll make it."

"Hope you can find your dancing shoes for tonight. Come on let's go for a swim." As they walked away Sophia explained to Jeff that night a large celebration on the beach in their honour was planned. Family would be coming from all around to celebrate their engagement. There was going to be music and dancing. Sophia winked at her fiancé.

They entered the ocean and felt cooled immediately. Every day in this place was just like living in paradise. Jeff felt better than ever and looked forward to an afternoon siesta with Sophia in his arms.

CHAPTER 7

J EFF BROOKS WATCHED the bonfire on the beach as it leapt towards the sky while Sophia clutched his arm beside him. Every time Jeff sat in front of a bonfire, it brought back memories of a camping trip after his mother passed away. She'd died at the hands of his lifelong friend Cory. Cory had visited him in his dreams during his siesta earlier in the day.

The dream was vivid: He was trapped inside a coffin, buried alive. As he clawed relentlessly at the coffin's interior fabric, it tore away to reveal bleeding flesh. Blood dripped down on his face like Chinese water torture. Each drop felt like battery acid. There was no choice; he had to continue to pull away the wet substance if he wished to get out. As he opened the flesh more, blood ran down his arms faster. The coffin filled with so much blood, Jeff feared he would drown. Then suddenly, a hand pulled him up through the fleshy wall. Cory smiled and laughed a heartily familiar laugh.

"You see Jeff, you did what you had to do, and you got what you wanted. We are no different." Cory's face melted from the heat. Jeff looked around at their surroundings to see the flames of hell. His body seared with pain from the heat. He could feel pinpricks of pain as he stared at his right arm.

Jeff woke from his siesta panicked, drenched with sweat and sore from the boar hunt. His right arm prickled with pain from sleeping on it awkwardly. He wished with all his heart to stop the scrapbook of flashbacks and nightmares of his past. No matter how he tried, he couldn't, they were just too fresh and painful. It felt as if an angry spirit kept tormenting him.

Jeff was Sophia's hero. Her fiancé had survived the hunting expedition with her father and more important, he had come back intact. She had down played the dangers of boar hunting to her future husband. She did this in part because she enjoyed the strong bond being created between Jeff and her father. The other part she couldn't acknowledge: that deep down, unconsciously, every girl wants to marry a man who has similar characteristics to her father. Four months ago a previous boar-hunting story scared the entire family. Her father had cornered a ninety-kilogram boar next to a cavern and the boar had immediately killed two of his dogs with its long tusks. The third dog was whipped around like a rag doll latched onto the hind leg of the boar. The boar was close to a steep slope and when Al approached the boar to stick the pig (as he called it). The dog let go. The animal and Al went rolling down the slope. As soon as Al regained his footing and stood up to find the boar, he was lanced in the back of the thigh by a tusk. Al turned around and fired his revolver, killing the boar. Working on adrenalin, he eviscerated the animal and carried it back to his truck. Only once he was sitting in the truck did Al notice the damage caused to his leg and his boot full of blood. He shoved a rag into the wound and tied his belt around it to hold it in place. When he made it back to his farmhouse, he had Maria pour alcohol into the wound and tie it off. He never sought medical attention and never stopped working. Jeff had some really big shoes to fill.

Jeff forced himself to look away from the fire and enjoy his surroundings. There must have been eighty people on the beach and it seemed that still more were showing up every hour. Sophia's family contained some very talented musicians. The music and dancing were hypnotic. While Jesus and Garcia played guitar, a quartet of singing aunts and uncles sang ballads from the past. Sophia managed to drag Jeff to the dance floor. He watched her move as she danced and felt his body flush with excitement. God he loved this woman. She was as levelheaded as she was beautiful. When she looked at him, she made him feel like nothing in his life would ever go wrong again. The music stopped and Jeff wandered over to get a couple of drinks for them.

A muscular man almost his own height was standing next to Al and stretched out his hand as Jeff approached. Jeff shook it and said "Hola."

Al made the introductions. "Jeff, this is my cousin Luis. He's agreed to take on the project you'd requested. He tells me that there will be no problem finding labourers and skilled tradesmen to build you and Sophia's dream home over by the beach."

Jeff was overjoyed. They hammered out a deal that would see Luis receive $300 a month for his foreman skills while all other tradesmen and labourers got $100. This was pocket change for Jeff who had a van with a floor full of money.

The men agreed to keep as much of the work in the family as possible. Al agreed to set up a shantytown of sorts for the workmen on his land. They would begin carrying rocks down from the hills at dawn. Everything seemed to be falling into place nicely.

Just then, a laughing Sophia grabbed Jeff by the waist and pulled him back to the dance floor. She was his Mexican goddess in every way. This truly was how life should be, thought Jeff. He couldn't wait to share a bed in the same house with his beautiful bride. For now, the spare bedroom down the hall in the Martinez home would have to do.

CHAPTER 8

TRUE TO HIS word, Luis gathered a crew together for the construction of Jeff's homestead. He examined the house plans on a makeshift table next to the previous night's bonfire that was still smouldering. A cool morning breeze danced through the men's hair as Lucky snored softly beneath the table. When Luis attempted to pronounce Jeff's name, it always sounded like Heff which made Jeff chuckle. Truthfully, Jeff began to feel like Hugh Hefner. "Heff, I understand and see no problem with any of these plans. One question though? Off the main bedroom there is a room with no door, next to the closet. What is that?"

"Luis, I was wondering when you were going to notice my little secret. That, my friend, will be a hidden compartment with a door that will look like a bookcase. Can you do that for me? Complete with a bookcase?" Jeff smiled one of his friendliest smiles.

"That is a wonderful idea Heff. Every man needs a place to call his own." Luis laughed heartily, deep from his stomach.

Jeff nodded, "Luis, please make sure that there is room for a safe." It was Luis's turn to nod. Jeff continued,

"Gather the men around at break time. I would like to pay them all in advance to let them know how happy I am to have them working on this project." Luis's jaw dropped, as Jeff placed $300 into the palm of his hand.

Jeff stood on the table and looked at the forty men gathered around him. He spoke slowly and deliberately to the men, not just because his Spanish was weak, but also to let the men know just how important this project was to him. "Men! Every man has a dream. My dream is to marry my beautiful Sophia and to have a wonderful home full of love and full of children." Some of the men with five or six children chuckled as Jeff carried on. "For this reason, even though we have just started, I will be paying you all today." The men roared their approval. Jeff felt like a king speaking to his people as Luis walked around and paid them one hundred American dollars.

As the excitement died down, Jeff bellowed. "I want to make myself very clear: Luis is in charge. What he says goes. While you are on the Martinez' land, you will show respect to the family and to their property. We will not tolerate any violence in the camp. You will be fed every day. If you can't follow these rules, you will be asked to leave. Do you understand?" The men stood in silence. Jeff asked again. "I said, do you understand?" This time the men roared, "yes" to his question. Jeff fed off the energy of the group. "Can you build me my dream?" The men roared 'YES' to his question. "Can you do it in time for our wedding, five months from today?" The men did not shout yes quite as strongly to this question. "Can you do it in five months if there is a two-month bonus to your salary upon completion?" The men roared, "yes" to this question with excited energy.

The men worked at an alarming rate for over a month. Long beams of timber were carted down from the hills and milled by hand. Most of the structure was framed and the masons had begun to sort out their stones. Luis and his crew handled most of the technical work. Everything was moving smoothly until one day, tragedy struck and the project was dealt a heavy blow.

CHAPTER 9

IN THE EARLY morning, a circular saw whined as it cut notches into a beam. Luis could tell that the blade needed to be changed, but they were still waiting for the shipment from the city. Luis was the perfect foreman since he had the most experience, owned and operated most of the power tools on the construction site. He stood thirty feet in the air on makeshift scaffolding as it swayed in the strong wind. At that moment a gust rocked the scaffold and the circular saw in Luis's hand bucked as the blade unnaturally twisted in the beam. The torque was too powerful for Luis to hold the saw in place. It jumped out of the beam and ran across Luis's left hand. His index and middle fingers fell to the ground like wood chips. He stared down at his hand in disbelief as his ring finger also dangled by a thread of skin. Blood poured out from where his fingers used to be, soaking the wood below.

The men around Luis quickly took action. They moved with lightning speed as they assisted him back to the ground. Jeff was alerted of the accident and came running to his project manager. "How bad is it?" He asked.

Luis still had the courage to smile at Jeff. "It's just a

flesh wound. Martello, give me your knife." He grabbed the knife and proceeded to lop off the remaining ring finger. He wrapped the hand tightly in a shirt and gave his last order for the day. "Heff I'll be back. Get me to the clinic Martello." They rushed to a vehicle and sped off.

Jeff couldn't believe the turn of events he'd just witnessed. "Why did he cut off his finger?" He asked to no one in particular.

One of Luis's best workers explained. "That is exactly what the doctor would have done. Luis knew that he was in shock and in no pain, that's the best time to do it. Forty minutes from now, when he reaches the clinic, the pain will be unbearable."

Jeff still didn't understand. "But they could've reattached the fingers over by the house that were left behind. We should've put them on ice and sent them with him."

The man laughed at this notion. "My friend, you are forgetting where you are. There is no such technology in these parts. The medicine is crude. The doctors do what they can with the supplies that are available." Jeff was frustrated as he walked away. He'd just lost his project manager and felt guilty that his friend had lost his fingers.

Work continued on the house as scheduled for the day. Jeff wandered around the workers' camp in the evening to check on morale. He was astonished when a vehicle pulled up and out stepped Martello, who then assisted Luis out of the passenger seat. The men cheered at his return. There was no left arm in the sleeve. Jeff thought the worst. "God, they amputated his whole arm."

Upon closer inspection Jeff realized the arm was inside his shirt. Luis made his way over to Jeff with assistance. Jeff immediately closed the distance. "Luis, what are you doing here?"

"Heff, I have a house to finish. If you'll still have me?" Luis barely had the strength to smile.

Jeff nodded his head. "Of course Luis. There is nothing wrong with your brain. How bad is your hand?" That is when Luis raised his shirt and Jeff stared in disbelief. Luis's hand had been surgically inserted into his abdomen. Jeff couldn't keep the shock out of his voice. "What the hell did they do to you?"

"An excellent way to stave off infection. There are no bandages to change. I'll still be able to work. The body heals itself." Luis smiled with effort.

"Luis, I want you to rest for as long as it takes for you to get your strength back."

Jeff still couldn't believe it. He brought Luis over to his tent and laid him down on his cot. When no one was listening, Jeff leaned down and whispered to Luis. "I'll be giving you workman's compensation for your troubles because you deserve it."

"You are a good man Heff. I am lucky to know you. I will ask my cousin's son Armand to join us to pick up the slack. He is young, strong and a good worker." Luis answered.

Jeff left the tent more hopeful. The men's morale seemed to lift with the return of Luis. Everything should be okay.

CHAPTER 10

OPHIA CREPT INTO Jeff's bedroom with the stealthiness shared by the entire Martinez clan. He couldn't believe how quietly they could move. She gently stroked his body, making him jump to attention immediately. He whispered to Her. "Sugar, you know that I love you more than the air I breathe. This doesn't feel right and I don't want to piss-off your parents. I don't want to disrespect them."

"My parents are out and my brothers are working in the barn, sleepyhead. It's already eight o'clock." Sophia persistently teased him with her hands.

Jeff had finally returned to more normal sleeping habits. The visits from Cory lessened as each day passed. He resisted the temptation to pin Sophia to the bed and give her what she wanted. "Sophia, I've been thinking. We know that the sex between us is unimaginably fantastic. So, I propose that we stop until our wedding day." A tear rolled down Sophia's cheek. Jeff asked, "What is it? What's wrong?"

"That is the most romantic thing I've ever heard. I love you more every day." Sophia embraced him.

After a few moments of sexual tension they separated

and Sophia announced. "Your breakfast is waiting for you on the table your majesty."

Jeff laughed. "My queen, I do not deserve thy royal treatment. Thank you. I am going to wash up and be right there." He joined Sophia at the large wooden farm table. The sun shone through the window, making Sophia's hair radiate. "I wanted to ask you your opinion about what to do about Luis. He seems to need to recover, but he also needs to work. I want to give him some money for his injured hand. What do you think?" He could see the wheels turning as she calculated her response. Sophia always took her time to answer really challenging questions. Jeff loved speaking with her.

"I think that is an extremely generous offer. Quite frankly, not something that he would expect." She replied very diplomatically.

"Would he be insulted? Would he feel that I was trying to buy out my remorse?"

Sophia replied quickly this time. "Although Luis is very skilled, his family is large and poor. It is nearly impossible for him to earn enough to feed his family. Any compensation given to him will lift his entire families' spirit." She sighed at the end.

Jeff asked one more question. "Also, before I forget. What do you know about Armand?"

Sophia smiled. "Armand and I grew up together. He is my cousin. I've not seen him in years. He has been helping Luis's family make ends meet for a while. You are doing so much for my family honey. I love you!"

"I love you too. Then it's settled. I'll go speak to Luis right now." Jeff kissed her softly.

Jeff wandered out into the extreme heat of the

morning and found Luis sitting in the shade monitoring the job site. The look on his face was that of a man who wished he was up on the scaffold swinging a hammer. Luis stood as Jeff approached. "Please, Luis, sit. Now Luis, what I am about to say comes from the heart. I won't take "no" for an answer and I will be personally insulted if you refuse my offer." Luis looked like a man who was about to lose his job. "Luis, I am very sorry to see you in pain and I want to make it up to you and your family."

Luis was about to explain how stupid he felt for allowing this to happen, when Jeff pulled out an envelope with $9,500.00 and placed it into Luis right hand. When he looked at the contents of the envelope this very tough man shed a tear that rolled down his cheek. The entire financial burden he felt as he sat in the chair only moments ago vanished. Luis choked up when he spoke. "Heff, I am not sure you know how much this means to me. I can never repay you. Thank you."

Jeff floated on air as he walked away from Luis. He was finally understanding some of the life lessons his mother tried to teach him in his teenage years. She would tell him that you can't light someone's path without lighting your own. He finally understood what that statement meant. Giving money to Luis for his pain and suffering made Jeff feel like a better man. His budding new life he'd created for himself shone as brightly as the sun.

CHAPTER 11

THE FRAMING ON the home was complete and the organization of stonework looked flawless. Jeff was totally amazed at the quality of labour. As most of the men were related to the Martinez family their work was not only a labour of pride, but also a labour of love. After a well-deserved day off, the next day's tasks involved milling the windows and doors. There was a natural flow since the men who'd completed the framing moved onto manufacturing window frames, door frames and milling the hardwood floors. Sophia's excitement grew with every moment. She felt just like a princess.

The men held a celebration to acknowledge their great achievement of staying on schedule. Jeff ordered in some beer and wine. He treated his employees the way he wished he'd been treated in the workforce. A man deserved to be treated like a man. Threaten a man with the loss of his livelihood, just like you would to a child with their favourite toy and you will have men who behave like children.

Sophia's brothers Garcia and Jesus were tending the bar for the event. Jeff left specific instructions not to let things get too out-of-control. Luis assured Jeff that all the men were on the same page. No one would be foolish enough to jeopardize their employment by drinking so much that they would be useless or bedridden tomorrow.

The men played cards and drank as they listened to some live music. Jeff had always been known for his wild parties and this one was no different. Sophia appeared next to Jeff with body language that showed urgency and distress. Jeff asked her, "What's going on?"

"It's my brothers. They're drunk and fighting." Sophia's face changed to embarrassment as she waved Jeff toward the bar.

"I should've specified that the bartenders not get pissed drunk. I never thought I had to worry about the twins. Welcome to the family!" Jeff thought to himself as he ran over to his future brothers-in-law.

The two men were rolling around on the ground in a bear hug. Some of the men gathered around to watch the entertainment. If ever there were two combatants that were equally matched, you'd figure twins were a good bet. Once Jeff arrived, a couple of the larger men grabbed Jesus, who seemed to be the aggressor, and one man grabbed Garcia who was laughing. He spat out, "you always were a pussy."

Jesus was fit to be tied and his response was the talk of the construction site for several months thereafter. Jesus looked at his identical twin brother and yelled. "You're an asshole and you're fucking ugly." All the men roared with laughter. This diffused the situation immediately. Jesus stormed off and Garcia continued to tend the bar.

Jeff gave Sophia an enquiring look to which she replied, "Those two are black and white. One is peaceful, the other violent. Every once in a while, the two forces collide like raging bulls."

CHAPTER 12

THE HOME LOOKED more complete each day. The clay roof was done and the doors and windows were installed. Luis accident hadn't slowed him down. In fact he seemed to work with more determination than ever. For this reason, Jeff was totally shocked when Luis made his request. "Heff, I must take a couple of days for my procedure at the clinic. They will be removing my hand and sewing up the opening. As I understand the doctor will want me close to the clinic until the skin dries out on my hand. Basically, my hand has been underwater for the last couple of months while the damage healed itself. During those critical few days I must keep the bandages clean and dry."

Jeff had no problem with this at all. In fact, there was maybe something Luis could do for him while in the city. "Luis, you take the time that you need. Armand has doubled productivity around here. He seems to have your knack for motivating the men. Are you going to drive there yourself?" Luis nodded his head yes. Jeff asked his favour. "Luis, if I was to give you a package to send to America, would you be able to ship it for me? It has to be sent through registered mail. The recipient will have to sign for the package. Have you ever sent anything that way before?"

"Every year at Christmas I send my sister a care package. She has never not received it." Jeff was relieved to hear Luis answer.

"When must you leave for the clinic?" Jeff had to figure out how much time he had.

"They are expecting me for tomorrow."

"Great, I'll have a package ready for you in a couple of hours."

Jeff raced up the steps of the Martinez family home. Lucky greeted him with happy tail wagging and hand-licking. Jeff opened the door and called out for Sophia. Just as he rounded the corner, he saw Jesus at the table clipping his nails and piling them on the vinyl tablecloth. Jeff's entire body shivered. Jesus spoke in a slow drawl. "Sophia just left for a walk. Can I help you? You look like you've seen a ghost."

Jeff stammered for a moment and regained his composure. "I need a small box for a package, a box for bank cheques or something around that size. Any idea where I might find one?"

Jesus walked over to an antique roll top desk and pulled out exactly that. "Here you go. That's good service, right?"

"Jesus, you are a good man. Thank you." Jeff loved how some things seemed to come together so perfectly. Like they were meant to be.

Jeff sat down on the porch with Lucky curled up at his feet and began writing. He wrote without stopping, the words flowed like water. Something that felt this right was meant to happen. He slipped the contents into the package, and sealed it tightly with packing tape. He wrote the name and address on the brown paper covering the box. He flipped it over and finished it off by adding the short form of the Junction City Four, JC4.

Jeff patted Luis on his back as he sent him on his way. "Drive safe, Luis. Take care of that package. Don't forget to listen to what the doctor tells you."

CHAPTER 13

A L SAT QUIETLY on the porch watching the hustle and bustle of construction in the distance. He'd never imagined this level of happiness for his daughter, let alone happiness spreading throughout his entire extended family. One rich American changed everything. Cousins and nephews who struggled to find employment were making enough money to survive for the next several years.

Jeff had been causing quite a stir in their little town. People made special trips to say hello. Some were people that Al and Maria had not seen in years. They enjoyed their sudden celebrity status and welcomed all the townspeople with open arms. Some days were busier than others, but for the most part the farm had become a meeting place for the town.

At first Al didn't think anything of the large black Land Rover with tinted windows as it approached the Martinez home. Until he noticed the government plates and two impeccably dressed men step out and approach. Al stopped relaxing immediately.

"Afternoon Señor Martinez. It's a lovely day for

construction work. An impressive building, I might add." the taller of the two men spoke.

"Yes, yes! It's a beautiful home for my daughter and her future husband. What brings the government to my doorstep?" Al's nerves of steel kept his face calm and polite.

"Señor Martinez, I fear the modest home you are constructing for your daughter will raise your taxes considerably, not to mention the fines you will incur for lack of proper permits. Now with proper payment today we could easily misplace our findings." The tall man carried the conversation, while the shorter one snapped photos and took notes.

"Let me discuss this with my future son-in-law. Please wait here." The taller man simply nodded. Above all else Al hated the leeches and bloodsuckers of society.

Al found Jeff who was going over the job site with Luis and quickly explained the situation. "So how much do they want?" Jeff asked

"Let's give them each $100 and we will be rid of them." Al quickly said.

"Done. Make sure they give you their names before you give them the money." Jeff nodded and pulled out the bills.

"Gentlemen, I have good news for you. I have your money. I'll just need to see some identification and you can be on your way." Al grimaced at this request as he walked back to the government vehicle.

The two government employees looked at each other indifferently and quickly pulled out their identification. Al examined the taller man's government credentials. "Señor Calderone." He placed the bill on the identification and handed it back. The shorter man also presented his credentials, "Señor Gonzola." Al handed him money as well. The two men were excited to see the American money.

They genuinely thanked Al for his time and drove off.

'That is definitely not the last we see of those two.' Al thought to himself.

CHAPTER 14

ALTHOUGH JEFF HAD the majority of the Martinez clan on a payroll, he still felt the need to contribute in other ways. He'd taken a lot of gentle ribbing at the dinner table over the last several months. Maria would often nudge Al and comment on when Jeff would provide the chicken for the roast. Sophia and her two brothers would laugh. Jeff never let it show how much this got under his skin. Basically, the family was saying that this all-American city man could never kill a chicken for the Sunday roast. Today the challenge would be met and conquered.

"Jeff, take the chickens on the right in the separate pen because they have been meat fed for the last month." Al gave the instructions.

"What do they normally get fed?" Jeff asked many questions.

"They are essentially fed food that makes them produce more eggs. Therefore if you kill the wrong chicken it won't taste right." Al loved his inquisitive mind. Jeff reached down and grabbed one of the plumper chickens.

Sophia was hiding just out of sight observing her man

in action. She knew how much doing this bothered Jeff. She promised to make it up to him on their wedding day. Their break from sex was proving to be very hard.

Jeff took a firm hold of the bird's neck and lowered it to the chopping block. His mind swirled with memories as he held the axe. He raised the sharpened steel high above his head and looked down at his target. At the precise moment when he lowered the axe to strike, Cory screamed in agony inside his mind. The axe made contact with the block with a thump. It took all of Jeff's strength to focus on his results. The bird had stopped squawking, that was a good sign. He felt no pain, another good sign. He let go of the bird and it took off running. Jeff hadn't expected this. The bird was running around the pen without a face. All that remained on the chopping block was a beak and a set of eyes. Blood poured out of the chicken's face as Jeff regained his composure and came back to the situation.

The first thing he heard was the laughter. The suddenly laughing audience made Jeff feel very unstable. He did what he'd been taught when you make a mistake, you correct it and prove people wrong. With lightning quick reflexes he grabbed another chicken from the pen and lopped its head off in the blink of an eye. He hung the gyrating bird by its feet on the fence. The laughter had stopped. He walked over to the faceless chicken that had run out of steam, brought it over to the block and lopped off the rest of its head. He hung it on the fence as well.

"Let's invite Luis over for the next roast. Seems like we have an extra chicken." As Jeff exited the pen, he felt a little ashamed of killing two chickens instead of one. He patted Al on the shoulder on his way out.

CHAPTER 15

MICHAEL THOMSON DRANK his coffee in large gulps inside the Tattoo You on the main strip in Junction City. This morning he whistled softly to himself as he prepared the paints and needles for his first client. Jack Armstrong's tattoo would be the most intricate and bizarre he'd ever done, not to mention the most profitable. Michael couldn't believe Jack's idea for a tattoo when he first walked through the door. After many lengthy discussions and explanations of his lifelong commitment to this kind of tattoo, Michael finally agreed to do it after hearing that seven other artists had turned down Jack and that money was no object. Jack was a rich man who enjoyed living on the edge with money to burn.

The bell above the door tinkled as Jack stepped in. This tattoo had taken months to complete and now Michael was merely adding colour. Jack walked into the back room, took off his shirt, said a quick hello and lay down on the massage table. There was never a lot of chitchat with Jack. Michael selected his colour and started up the needle. Every time he worked on this piece, he still couldn't believe it. The border of the tattoo was a series of chained skulls surrounding a full size Ouija board complete with stars, "yes", "no", numbers, alphabet and "goodbye". Michael had even managed to give the skin the look of a textured playing board surface. It amazed him but it was also the scariest thing he'd ever created. Even for a full-fledged member of the Goth society this tattoo was off the charts.

When the doorbell tinkled yet again, Michael jumped. Ever since he lost all of the Junction City four crew, his nerves just weren't the same. Michael excused himself and checked on the visitor. He stood there, shocked to see his mother standing in the parlour. Quickly he snapped the curtain shut. If her devout Catholic eyes were to fall upon his latest creation, it would trigger a phlebitis episode that would create a lifetime of guilt for Michael. "Mom, what an unexpected surprise." He gave her a peck on the cheek as he squeezed her hands. His mother was always easily excitable so he could tell there was something pressing.

"Michael, a package came for you today in the mail. It was marked urgent so I rushed it right over." She flipped the package end over end on the counter as her face pleaded for Michael's full attention. She handed it to him.

He flipped it over and read JC4. This couldn't be. He hid his excitement from his mother and whispered to her. "Mom, thanks a lot for this. I'm sure it's nothing. I've got a very important client in the back I need to attend to." His mom acknowledged her son's busy schedule and waddled her large frame back to her car. As soon as she was out of sight, he tore open the package. Jack's Ouija board could wait.

The $10,000 bundle of cash fell out of the package into his hand. He could feel his eyes growing larger and his blood pressure rising. He put the money back in and pulled out the letter, which said:

Michael,

You look like you need a vacation. Stop scribbling on people and come soak up some rays. I'm getting married and I need a best man. There is only you. Please come. I am in Zempoala, Mexico. It's a small coastal town nestled near the slopes of the Sierra Madre Oriental mountain chain, which parallels the Gulf Coast in central Mexico. I need you here before October 27th. Use the money to fly into Vera Cruz, Mexico. And then rent or buy a 4x4. You'll need it. You can't say no, and we have so much to talk about.

See you soon, Jeff.

Michael stuffed the package into his lunch bag and went back to finish up Jack's tattoo. His mind raced. "Maybe" he thought, "maybe."

CHAPTER 16

JEFF AND SOPHIA stood in front of their brand-new two-storey, stone house. It was absolutely breathtaking. Luis and his crew had finished early, just as he had predicted. Armand was worth his weight in gold. He served as a second foreman during the build. Luis walked up behind the couple and gave them a warm embrace. His damaged hand had recovered nicely. He had still lost three fingers on his left hand in the accident, but at least there was no need for further amputation. The nubs of his fingers were salmon pink in colour. "The happy couple. Heff, you are a very lucky man. There are still a few touch ups going on inside, but the house is basically finished. The men have planned a celebration in your honour."

"Luis, you've made us so happy. The celebration should be in honour of you and your men." Jeff gave a huge sigh.

"When should we move in?" Sophia snuggled in closer to Jeff.

Jeff weighed the family traditions heavily. "As much as I would have you in that house tomorrow, you and I both know your parents would be very disappointed in us if we didn't wait. Besides it's only another month. For now I can sleep in the spare bedroom until our wedding. After we'll enter the master bedroom together and. . . ." They all giggled along with Sophia.

Luis went ahead and informed the men of the festivities for the evening. Jeff went over to the van that was nestled next to the pigpen. It had been months since he'd slept in the van. He preferred the Martinez home. The van had cover from the crops behind it. The pigpen was to his left and only the right remained unprotected from prying eyes. No one seemed to be observing him as he lowered the bumper and inserted the two keys into the iron panel. He removed the panel and grabbed two $10,000 bundles to pay the men their bonuses. Quickly he replaced the panel and the bumper. Jeff stood and turned, seeing Armand right behind him. Jeff felt his insides move in slow motion and then speed up, slamming in a lurch in his rib cage. The blood inside his temples created a slow steady thump.

"Armand, I trust that you'll tell no one what you've seen!" He swallowed and spoke with purpose.

"Tell anyone what? Jeff, we all owe you a great deal of thanks. The last thing I would ever do is to jeopardize what we have. Everyone has secrets. Even me." Armand kept his eyes locked on Jeff.

"That means the world to me Armand. I hope you will visit us often. There should be some little second cousins running around here before long." Jeff relaxed a little.

"Take good care of Sophia. She is a good woman. The day you take her for granted is the day we'll have a problem. Since you seem to be an honourable man, that day will never come." Armand nodded, smiled and kissed Jeff on both cheeks and left.

Jeff felt uneasy about the whole situation. The quicker he could get the money into the house safe the better he'd feel.

CHAPTER 17

JEFF WOKE UP in the guest bedroom of his new house. He stared at the beautiful craftsmanship inside the room. Each one of the bedrooms had rich mahogany hand-carved molding around the windows and doors. From this room the ocean could be seen in the distance. Primarily, the view consisted of the Martinez homestead, two hundred feet away.

Jeff felt a chill as he slipped out from under the covers. He walked down the long crafted mahogany hallway to the guest washroom; keeping his promise to Sophia that the master suite would be off limits until their wedding day.

Jeff and Sophia opted to live off nature's resources as much as possible. Their hot water system sat on the south-facing side of the home, where fencing protected two large 500-gallon black storage tanks. They were filled by the rain and heated by the sun. During the dry season when the rain came less frequently, the tanks would be filled with well water. Since the dry season meant extreme heat, the cool well water from the ground would almost frost the pipes. Those pipes ran beneath the home and fans blew the coolness from the pipes throughout the house. This would act as a natural air conditioner. In the winter months Jeff's backup plan for hot water was a wetback system that he'd remembered from his youth. The wood-fired stove had water pipes looped behind it, creating hot water. Therefore, when the fire warmed the hearth of the home, it also heated the water. He wasn't convinced that they would have hot water year round, but the idea was sound.

Jeff's early morning shower with six jets hitting his body and copious amounts of hot water proved to be a success. Everything seemed to work. The water from the showers and sinks flowed into a grey water tank used to fill toilets and water the gardens. The fan and the lights were powered by large solar panels on the roof. The system came with a sensor that pivoted the panels as the sun moved across the sky. When he stepped out of his hot shower and looked into the large mirror it was completely clear. This was possible because of the hot water pipes that looped behind the bathroom mirror on its way to the shower, heating the mirror to eliminate steam.

During his morning routine he thought about all the obstacles they'd encountered and overcome. Luis had finally found a middle man, or in this case a middle company. It proved to be very hard to pay for large items in cash without creating a lot of questions. So they found a company that bought the items for them. When their stock came in, he sent Luis to the city with a truck and paid the construction company in cash, and an extra 10 percent not to ask any questions.

Jeff walked through his dream home like a child on Christmas day. He stepped into his private area off the master bedroom suite and reached for the autobiography of Sir Winston Churchill. One slight pull of the book and the whole unit swung out exposing the safe room. He rotated the dial, set the tumblers and turned the handle. The heavy safe door swung open exposing its treasure. Jeff stared proudly at his $450,000 of leftover cash. He'd done very well for himself spending around $250,000 so far. Considering his past history, the fact that he was still alive was a miracle. His heart nearly stopped as he heard the banging on the front door. He locked up the safe and raced to the entrance.

"I can't believe you're alive." Jeff opened the door and felt utterly weightless as Michael Thomson spun him in the air like a child. Michael was yelling with joy.

"Thank God you're here. Let's get some beers. We've got a lot to talk about." Salty tears rolled down his cheeks freely once Michael set him down. He hadn't realized how much he had missed his friend and it caught him by surprise. He slapped Michael on his back.

CHAPTER 18

"**H**OW DID YOU enjoy the trip here?" Jeff chuckled as he asked the first question. Jeff and Michael sat down on a fine Corinthian leather sofa surrounded by handcrafted mahogany molding and furniture. They each gave welcoming smiles and cracked open their ice-cold beers.

"Well as you can tell, airline seats still aren't made for me. The seat next to me was empty, so I wasn't meant to feel bad about my size. Once we landed, I felt like part of the Amazing Race. Find a vehicle, find a map, find food and figure out how to navigate to a little town that no one knows exists. Other than that, piece of cake." Michael laughed from his diaphragm and adjusted his considerable weight on the sofa.

Michael continued. "Talk about a turn of events. One minute we're together in Junction City and the world around us is changing rapidly and the next second you've disappeared. That's one story I've been waiting to hear. I've missed you man. What happened?" Jeff handed him another beer and felt an angry spirit creeping into his thoughts. He fought the anger and smiled.

Jeff let the silence hang as he remembered the

nightmares from those days that seemed so long ago and yet, still fresh. "Where should I start? You know that Cory killed my Emily, my mom, Chris, John McCork and Frank?" Michael only nodded not wanting to interrupt. "Well, a couple of days before he died, I discovered his pantry in the sky."

"I'd heard about that in the papers from my mom." Michael nodded and pointed at Jeff.

Jeff continued. "Well I found that pantry in the sky and that's when I knew Cory had been my worst enemy and my best friend, all rolled into one. So I staged Cory's standoff in front of the hospital. I broke his back with an axe, glued a gun to his hand and told him that he had to confess to make everything between us right." Michael was speechless. Jeff continued. "You look shocked. It's just everyday stuff. It happens to everyone, doesn't it?" Jeff took a large breath and yawned to keep from crying. "I even confronted Fred Blake before I left. That bastard wouldn't even acknowledge that maybe they were the cause of Cory's problems. I hit him a good one and left. But now . . . now I am in, opposite land. My world has righted itself. Everything is perfect."

"Jeff, originally I was royally pissed that you left. Now I can't blame you. I was mad because no one came to my defense. You were gone and my mom's word that I wasn't Cory's accomplice wasn't enough for the police. They kept me locked up for three weeks, all because Cory planted evidence from John's murder in my room. They grilled me for days after. Asking questions like; what were my whereabouts for this date, who was my alibi, did I know what Cory was up to? You name it, they asked it. A couple of those dates I was with you and you were gone.

I thought you were dead. My appointed lawyer just kept telling me to cooperate and that if I stopped the cops were going to press charges. He said there was enough circumstantial evidence to convict me, but the cops didn't believe I was involved. It was all surreal. Eventually they let me walk out. That experience changed my outlook on life. I started looking at things with a more open mind." Michael got up and stretched his legs and admired the view of the ocean.

Jeff stood, stunned. He never knew how much Michael had suffered. He patted Michael on the back and handed him another beer. "Come on upstairs I'll give you the tour." Michael listened as they walked. He told him all about Sophia, her parents, hunting with her dad, the house and finally he dropped the bomb. That heavy weight he'd been carrying inside him. The only secret the Junction City Four ever had. "Remember that settlement I received from that Kansas City bank? I had physiotherapy for my arm? Well, the bank robber was Cory and I was his accomplice." Like a proud child with a new toy Jeff opened the secret safe room. The safe opened smoothly and unveiled the money. Michael held the wall for support and couldn't speak.

CHAPTER 19

"**I**S THIS WHY Cory murdered Chris?" Michael finally managed to ask the first question that stunned Jeff.

That had never even occurred to Jeff. "No, absolutely not. Cory and I didn't want to get you guys involved and we promised that our actions would never affect you guys. Cory killed Chris out of pure jealousy. He'd all these conspiracy theories in his head. He thought Chris and I were planning on cutting him out of the gang. Weird shit! Stuff you can't even make up. I think that's why he planted stuff in your room. I'd say you're lucky to be alive." Michael swallowed hard when he heard those words.

They quietly walked out of the room and stepped outside onto a terrace overlooking the ocean. Jeff asked Michael one of many favours to come. "If I send you back with some money, do you think you could take care of my mother's house? You'll be well compensated of course. You'd just need to hire someone for upkeep and pay the taxes. What do you think?"

"Of course. How about I rent it from you?" Michael agreed.

"How about you stay there for free." Jeff smiled.

"Well, if you insist." Michael laughed.

"I do insist. Anything for my best man. Speaking of that, you can't mention any of this to Sophia. She doesn't know about Cory. She only knows that something keeps me from sleeping at night." They shook hands on their deal.

"You ever going to tell her?" Michael wondered aloud.

"Not if I can help it. Right now she thinks I'm a rich boy whose family died. I'm someone looking to make a fresh start. Really that isn't that far off from the truth." Jeff rubbed his chin.

"All right. I'll tow the party line." Michael nodded.

In the distance Sophia came over a small dune of sand and approached the beautiful new home. "So, you are already entertaining without me. I really can't complain. I would do the same. I heard about the mysterious stranger and thought I should come over and see him with my own eyes." She walked over, introduced herself and shook his hand. Michael was clearly taken by her beauty.

"Now I understand everything. Jeff, you didn't tell me you were marrying the most beautiful woman in the world." Michael made Sophia blush.

"And she can cook." Jeff added. Sophia playfully slapped his arm.

"So tell me Sophia, are you aware you're marrying the greatest criminal mind from Junction City?" Michael chuckled and added. Jeff nearly choked on his beer. What the hell was he doing? Michael purposely avoided Jeff's eye contact. Sophia looked as stunned as Jeff. Michael continued. "So Jeff never told you about the time, he hid a cow in the principal's office in high school? That cow used the files as feed and the desk as an outhouse. Jeff never got caught. The principal was sorry to have crossed paths with Jeff Brooks. Or, how about the thirty chickens he released over at our rival school. They shut the place down for the afternoon because it caused such a problem."

Jeff had forgotten about Michael's sense of humour and cut him off. "Hey, hey, don't make it sound like I was by myself for all these pranks. If I recall, you were there beside me too." They were all laughing.

Next to arrive over the dune was Sophia's family, Al and Maria and Garcia and Jesus. They all enjoyed meeting the new stranger. Michael did his best with Spanish and when he couldn't Sophia would help translate. Jeff had been speaking only in Spanish around Sophia and she would speak only in English. It proved to be excellent way to learn for both of them.

It was Al's turn to share a story. "Garcia and Jesus were eight. The farm was really starting to function well. That is until Garcia and Jesus decided to tease my Brahma bull. I'd named it Tiny because it was the largest bull I'd ever seen. Who knows what these two boys were thinking?" He pointed to the twins and they hung their heads. "Tiny got himself all fired up and charged the boys who were on the other side of the fence. It tore through that fence like it was toilet paper. I screamed at the boys to take higher ground and thank God they did. They climbed that tree over there, faster than squirrels. Tiny went over to the pick-up truck and lifted it off the ground three feet with his horns. I ran in the house and grabbed my rifle. When I stepped out off the porch, I fired a shot into the air. Now most animals when they hear a loud explosion will duck for cover. Not a Brahma bull though. Tiny charged straight for me, more pissed off than ever, with car parts and tires hanging off his horns. I only had one shot and thank God I made it. Shot it right between the eyes. His momentum carried him almost to my feet. I went in and changed my underwear and that was the last bull we ever had on the farm." The story may not have been as funny, but it captivated the audience.

There were kisses and hugs all around as everyone headed off for their beds. As Jeff watched Sophia leave, he longed for her long legs and warm embrace.

CHAPTER 20

JEFF DREAMED AS he slept deeply. He sat in the center of the room surrounded by thousands of mason jars filled with nail clippings. His flesh seemed to crawl with a thousand different bugs. As he stared around in the distance and all he could see was endless lines of jars of nails. Out of nowhere, hanging upside down like a spider, he felt the awful breathe tickle the back of his neck. Cory's face was only inches away. The putrid smell of decaying flesh made his throat burn. Jeff vomited in his mouth and swallowed it down.

"Michael as your best man? You know that should be me. A true friend would never betray a blood brother." Cory spoke slowly as he remained hanging upside down.

"I owe you nothing. You owe me everything. I helped put you out of your misery. The world is safer without you." Jeff laughed in his face.

Cory's scream sounded like a thousand warriors heading to battle and he waved his hand over the jars. They burst into flames creating a smell of burning hair. That smell mixed in with Cory's decaying stench, made

Jeff want to vomit again. "Jeff, I gave you what you have today. Your second chance was created by me."

Jeff shook his head and covered his ears with his hands. When he did this, he shielded the extreme heat developing all around him. He felt his skin melting away. With lightning quick reflexes he grabbed Cory and threw him into the flames. That felt good. The moment didn't last though. Cory emerged from the flames, flesh burning and walked up to Jeff and gripped his arm. His grip was stronger than a mechanical vise and the heat from Cory's still burning hand seared his skin. Jeff screamed in agony and began to thrash wildly.

Jeff woke to someone shaking him. He thought that the angry spirit must have been tormenting him again. He was convinced that some sort of spirit was causing his frustrations and his anger. He heard a voice, Michael's voice. "Jeff, Jeff. Snap out of it. Holy crap. Are you okay?" Michael was standing next to his bed. Once again, Cory Blake had ruined a perfectly good night's sleep.

"Yeah, I'm good now. It was just a little visit from our friend. It must be the pressure of the big day. What time is it?" The sun was just peeking over the ocean. The sky looked clear. It was an excellent day to get married. Jeff got out of his drenched bed and drank water from the fridge. He wondered aloud to his best man. "At what point in my life will these nightmares go away?"

Michael didn't have the answer and just let the silence hang.

CHAPTER 21

THE HAPPY COUPLE and the priest stood on a platform as the ocean shimmered in the background. Jeff and Sophia stood in front of the local priest as he read out the vows. The scene resembled a Norman Rockwell painting; The Ocean waves lapped the shore rhythmically in the distance. Everything was perfect. All the relatives had remained on the property after the construction of the house. The construction shantytown had turned into a Martinez shantytown. Maria's side of the family seemed just as large as Al's. The Lomas family also held family traditions close to their hearts. There were tears throughout the crowd. The very simple service ended with a romantic kiss that Hollywood writers could never have envisioned. Fifty white doves were released and flew in formation as they circled the crowd of people. Family and friends clapped and cheered their approval.

If the newlyweds had their way, they'd have rushed into the new house not to reemerge for at least three days. Instead, they did the rounds of the two hundred and fifty guests. Many families had eight or more and it was assumed that the newlyweds would do their part to continue this tradition. Both Sophia and Jeff had simultaneous thoughts of getting started immediately.

Michael started the festivities with a speech that spoke of his friend as a mischievous youth who matured into a productive member of society, who made friends easily and who he admired and looked up to. There were more tears as he spoke of Jeff's mother and how she was surely watching over them now. Michael raised his glass to the happy couple and toasted their future. Jeff jumped up and hugged him.

Jeff then thanked everyone for coming and urged everyone to stay awhile. He'd never felt love like this in his life. The families danced and sang all night. The moonlight and torches lit the packed dance floor. Garcia and Jesus were enjoying themselves as they danced with another set of twins from the Lomas side of the family. Armand seemed to be holding court with several pretty women. Luis danced wildly with his wife and children, seemingly unaffected by his damaged hand. Al and Maria moved very fluidly as they danced. Everybody had a fantastic night.

As the evening wound down, Jeff and Sophia were being urged to leave and they obliged. Jeff carried Sophia over the threshold of their new home. They entered the master bedroom practically naked as they had already shed most their clothes in unabashed passion. For the first time in their lives they made love as a married couple. The sensation was ten-fold times better than any experience Jeff had before. It was the greatest night of his life. He rolled over and whispered into Sophia's ear. "I love you."

"I love you." She whispered back.

CHAPTER 22

A FEW WEEKS LATER Michael headed back to the airport. Even though he had thirty thousand in cash taped to his back, the trip turned out to be uneventful. When he returned to Junction City, he moved into Jeff's home and started making the appropriate payments for taxes, hydro and water, and hired a neighbour's son to cut the grass and rake the leaves.

One afternoon Michael sat watching the satellite dish on his big screen television. An aggressive knock on the door startled Michael from his leather Lazy-Boy chair. When he opened the door Chief Greg Mullen stood statuesque, with an impressive posture for a man his age. Michael invited him inside. Mullen cleared his throat and began. "I thought maybe Jeff had come back. Do you know where he is?" Michael hadn't thought of this when he took Jeff's offer.

"He went north up to Canada." Michael said.

"Whereabouts in Canada?" Mullen asked.

"Calgary, Alberta. He heard about the large need for all kinds of labourers. He'd had enough of Junction

City and sent me some money to take care of his mom's house." Michael replied.

Chief Mullen nodded. "It's good to hear that he's all right. After the whole incident with Cory . . . I'd figured the worst. Next time you speak to him let him know that there are no charges pending against him. We think he may have assaulted Cory just before his death, but the evidence doesn't warrant an arrest."

"I'll let him know that chief." Michael knew Jeff was guilty and didn't believe Chief Mullen. He'd watched enough television to know that the police never let someone getaway.

After Mullen left, Michael scribbled a letter to Jeff. The words were simple.

Jeff,

Mullen is still after you. The house is in good hands.

Your friend Michael,
JC4ever!

CHAPTER 23

JEFF AND SOPHIA spent hours together enjoying each other's company. She took up painting when she needed some alone time, and he finally took up surfing. He discovered peace and tranquility as the ocean rhythmically raised him up, then down, as he waited for the next wave.

Jeff bobbed in the ocean and thought of the festivities after their wedding that ended earlier in the month. Families had packed up and left for the lives they'd put on hold. He already missed Luis and Armand. They'd all become good friends. They were all very easy-going and that type of personality really appealed to Jeff's new lifestyle. Garcia and Jesus still seemed distant to him. Not that they didn't accept him, it was more like their personalities didn't fit his. Jeff's thoughts were pulled away as he gazed in the direction of his house.

A cloud of dust rose in the distance as a vehicle approached. The vehicle was close enough for him to recognize it and he raced toward the shore to intercept the intruders in the black SUV. They stepped out just as Jeff emerged from the salty water.

"How can I help you today?" He greeted them with a healthy bellow.

Señor Calderone spoke first. "Señor, a beautiful day for a surf. We came to speak of your lack of permits for this house."

"Well if I recall, last time you gentlemen were here you were paid handsomely to make those problems go away!" Jeff chuckled.

This time Gonzola spoke. "We are afraid that the new management in charge requires paperwork to be filed. Of course that costs money."

"More money? I'll get you more money inside. Wait here." Jeff could see where this was heading. He feared, however, that it would never end.

The two men smiled with greed. When Jeff emerged from the home he handed each man $100 and said, "Señor Gonzola, Señor Calderone, I trust you understand the perils of going too often to the well. If this persists, I'll have no money left."

The two men assured him the visits would be much less frequent now that the new management had been paid. Jeff had his doubts.

Sophia stepped out of the home as the vehicle left the Martinez's property. "Who was that?" Jeff kissed his beautiful wife. "That, my love, was your government hard at work."

Sophia's quick smile showed her disinterest for the conversation. "Well I have fantastic news that will make you forget all about that. Are you ready?" Jeff nodded. "Are you ready to be a Daddy?"

Jeff shouted with joy and picked her up. Then they sprinted into the ocean together. It had become their tradition. When they exited the ocean, Jeff grasped Sophia's hand. "Let's go and tell your parents the wonderful news."

When Sophia's parents saw their daughter dripping wet, they recognized the signs of good news. They celebrated the news with laughter and stories from childhood. Jeff loved every minute of his new life.

CHAPTER 24

NINE MONTHS SEEMED more like nine weeks. Jeff couldn't believe the day had arrived so quickly. He was about to be a father. He'd never felt more useless in his life as he listened to Sophia's cries of anguish from the next room. As they sat together, Al patted his knee in an effort to comfort him.

"She is in good hands Jeff. Maria is there and Antonella is the best midwife in all of Mexico. She's delivered hundreds of babies. In fact, she delivered most of the little Martinez's you saw running around and playing during your wedding. Relax. You are as white as a ghost."

Inside the room, Maria held her daughter in a partially seated position. When it came time to push, Maria held her daughter by the shoulders and massaged her back. Sophia screamed in pain as her perineum stretched and tore to make room for the baby's head. She already wanted the labour to be over, but the work had just begun.

Antonella listened to the baby's heartbeat with her stethoscope. The look of concern on her face did not provide any reassurance to Maria. Both women could tell that the labour was taking its toll on both mother and baby. They began screaming at Sophia that the time was now. She needed to give every ounce of energy she had on the next push. Sophia seemingly got the message, as her next push was enough to allow the baby's head and shoulders to slide out. Antonella worked quickly as the umbilical chord was wrapped around the infant's neck. She knew that this joyous occasion could turn to one of tragedy in the blink of an eye. She managed to get enough slack in the cord to free the infant. The women laughed and cried tears of joy.

Jeff stood on wobbly legs as he observed all the blood on the bed and his very pale wife. Sophia held their daughter in her arms, snuggled to her bare chest. Jeff did his best to hide the concern on his face.

"Say hello to Emily Maria." Sophia spoke in a whisper. Tears welled up in his eyes. He was so happy to hear that Sophia had accepted Emily as their daughter's name. The name was a tribute to his fiancé who was murdered by Cory.

"Hello Emily Maria. You caused your mommy a lot of stress over the last nine months. We're very happy you've finally arrived." Jeff whispered as well. He cut the umbilical cord where he was instructed to and Antonella took over. He was surprised by the toughness of the cord that had carried nutrients to his new child.

Jeff felt a tug on his arm as Al escorted him out of the room. He explained that the women would finish up with the afterbirth and other procedures on Sophia. He told Jeff, "It's best to let the ladies finish up in private. The baby is safe. Everything will be okay."

When the men re-entered the room, Maria beamed

with pride at her granddaughter's name. Al and Maria stood next to their daughter and her new baby as Jeff snapped a photo to capture this special day. Emily nursed greedily as both mother and daughter learned from each other. The moment would last forever in Jeff's mind. Each new beginning purged out old horrors.

CHAPTER 25

EMILY MARIA SEEMINGLY grew overnight, as did Jeff's abilities as a father. He quickly became the kind of father he wished he'd grown up with. Emily's soft blue eyes, olive skin and dark hair made her an instant star in the community. As described by everyone, she was a living doll. Jeff and Sophia joked that they were simply little Emily's entourage. They were there to make sure that the little princess had all her desires met as her fans showered her with praise.

Jeff stood behind Emily as she grasped his two fingers while she walked. She shouted and stomped her feet with excitement. The new parents brimmed with pride as they demonstrated their daughter's newfound talent. However, proudest of all were Al and Maria. They acted like teenagers who discovered love for the first time whenever Emily was around. Every time they saw their little Emily it was as if God himself had touched their hearts. Even Jesus and Garcia seemed to soften whenever Emily would squeeze their fingers or bite them on the nose.

Her first birthday had arrived in the blink of an eye. Jeff couldn't believe all the wonders he and Emily had discovered over the past year. All the butterflies, caterpillars, ants, and grasshoppers they'd chased. She had her first taste of sand. Luckily she had stayed well under the allowable one pound of sand per year.

Suddenly on that special day Emily had an extra twinkle in her eye as Jeff felt a tender peck on his cheek. Jeff turned and kissed Sophia on the lips. Emily giggled and clapped her hands. "Our number one fan." beamed Sophia.

"So do you think your parents have gone a little overboard?" Jeff laughed, as he looked around at the fifty-foot table with balloons and white tablecloth that gently blew in the afternoon breeze.

"Let them be. They are excited to have a grandchild they can spoil." Sophia smiled.

"Is that a white pony? Sophia, she's only one. At this rate when she turns twenty they'll have to buy her a fleet of sports cars and her own island." Jeff looked over at the field and couldn't believe his eyes.

"Since when are you concerned about spoiling our daughter?" Sophia chuckled quietly to herself.

In truth Jeff had been thinking about the longevity of his assets. There would come a time when he would need to refill his safe.

Just then, the black SUV pulled into the Martinez lane. Armand and Luis stood in front of the vehicle blocking its path. Gonzola and Calderone quickly stepped out of the vehicle. Jeff raced to the four men and stood in front of the two government workers. "Gentlemen, as you can see, you have come at a bad time. It is my daughter's first birthday. It's a family affair. You'll have to excuse my relatives. They are rather sensitive about exposing undesirables to my little princess." Jeff noticed that the two men were drunk. He reached into his pocket and palmed some money into each man's hand as he shook it. The men were satisfied and left.

When there was a lull in the party Jeff called over Armand, Luis, Jesus and Garcia. Jeff spoke with a certain edge in his voice. "Do you guys know anyone who can get us information on those two men? I want to know everything about them. Where they live, who they work for, if they are married, if they have children? Everything." The men knew where you could get that kind of information and it wouldn't be long before Jeff knew all he needed.

Emily blew out her first candle and received her first ride (with assistance from her protective dad) on her very own pony. Everyone beamed with joy as the little princess squealed with excitement.

CHAPTER 26

JACK ARMSTRONG'S APARTMENT in Kansas City was a bachelor's paradise. The Sub Zero fridge contained every alcoholic beverage known to man. The kitchen gleamed with stainless steel counters and appliances. This created a stark contrast against the glossy black tile and hanging halogen fixtures. The living area projected wealth and stature. The furniture in the penthouse loft was a mix of black leather and metal.

Jack lay face down in a prone position on his Persian rug. "Doom" and "Gloom" poured candle wax over the length of his body. Jack welcomed the pain. He'd met the two women at The Garden of Eden, a local mediaeval/ Gothic club. He knew those weren't their real names and quite frankly he didn't care. After months of extensive work on his tattoo he was finally going to find out if it had been worthwhile.

Doom and Gloom were both dressed in leather dominatrix outfits and both had bodies that would make any man beg. They walked around chanting as they placed large black candles in a pentagram formation. Next, they stroked his naked flesh with two black roses. He could feel the thorns scraping his skin and again, he welcomed the pain. As they chanted, the women slowly squeezed the rose stems more tightly. Thorns pierced their palms producing blood that dripped onto the Ouija board tattoo. As they traced the blood with their nails, the chanting filled the room.

The specially designed titanium heart-shaped tripod with German optical lens rested on his back. Doom and Gloom grew excited when the tripod seemed to practically race around their submissive client's back. At first they were frightened by the raw energy produced. Gloom commanded the presence. "Who are you, Most Powerful One?" The tripod seemed to stop, almost as if the spirit was contemplating whether or not it should waste time with these simple bags of flesh and bone. Finally the tripod moved beneath the women's hands stopping over each letter, C-O-R-Y.

"How old are you?" Doom asked and the answer came quickly, 26.

"Are you evil?" Gloom asked. The answer, YES.

"Did you kill people?" Doom asked. The answer, YES.

The tool began to move wildly unprovoked in a repetitive pattern. J-C-4, J-C-4, J-C-4, J-C-4, M-I-C-H-E-A-L, C-O-M-E 2 M-E, M-I-C-H-E-A-L, C-O-M-E 2 M-E, J-E-F-F-C-O-M-E 2 M-E, J-C-4, J-C-4, J-C-4, J-C-4.

The candles began to flicker as the air grew colder. Suddenly, the candles blew themselves out, throwing the room into darkness. The sounds of heavy breathing were broken as Gloom stumbled for the light switch. The lights in the room blinded everyone.

"That was awesome. When can we do it again?" Doom shrieked in her excitement.

"That's enough for tonight. You've got to leave now. Come on, get your stuff and get out!" Jack Armstrong felt more alive than he ever had before. His body coursed with electricity as he shoved the vixens out into the apartment hallway. Their curses of dissatisfaction meant nothing to him. He raced into his washroom and examined himself in the mirror. Every muscle in his body flexed. He felt out of control. At once, for no apparent reason he examined his hands, more specifically, his nails. The washbasin drawer slid open smoothly and he lifted out a pair of nail clippers. His face resembled an anguished weight lifter as he clipped each fingernail. With each clip he grew calmer. Once the task of clipping all his nails had been accomplished he held the clippings in his hand like someone searching for loose change. The same force that raged before brought Jack to the kitchen and he placed the clippings in a jar. Waves of calm and ecstasy washed over him as he collapsed on the tiled floor.

CHAPTER 27

ICHAEL WORKED ON a remembrance piece on a young lady who'd just lost her grandfather. He loved this part of the job. Many of the stories behind people's tattoos were very heartwarming. This young woman's grandfather had raised her after her abusive, drug addict mother left town to become a prostitute in Kansas City. The portrait of her grandfather with dates below was an excellent tribute to the man she honoured and loved. With her grandfather's guidance she paid for college on her own and thrived in school. She told him about her graduation and her new grade school teaching job she started last month. It was nice to here how she loved every minute of her day.

Her mother had died when she was only ten years old. Her pimp shot her in broad daylight in the wild slums of Kansas City. She told Michael how her poor grandfather had paid for her mother's tombstone and burial. Every year he brought her to the gravesite at the Junction City Memorial Cemetery and they paid their respects. He'd say these words to her, "Love your mother with all your heart. Hatred is too easy. She was your mother, the woman who brought you into this world. Without her, you would not exist. She was not perfect . . . and none of us are. Learn from her mistakes. You only get one body, one mind, and one soul. Take care of it."

The cash register rang its bell as Michael thanked the girl for allowing him to be a part of her special tattoo. As she left the shop, a very happy Jack Armstrong entered the door. He exclaimed excitedly, "It works!"

Michael did not make the connection immediately. "Michael, the tattoo you did on my back, it works!" Jack clarified on a more serious tone.

"That's great Jack. I'm glad to hear the good news." For some reason Michael had never expected Jack to actually use the crazy tattoo. Michael had never done any tattoo of that nature, so he chose his words wisely.

Jack continued carefully. "The very first spirit that contacted us spelled out your name Michael. Can you believe it? Your name! I had to come and tell you. I'm assuming that since you did all the artwork, there must be some weird connection don't you think?"

Michael was speechless. He simply nodded.

Jack tried to explain a bit more. "Tell me, do the letters J-C-4 mean anything?" Michael simply nodded.

"How about the name "Cory"?" Jack enjoyed Michael's freaked out expression.

"J-J-Jack you got to stop. Cory murdered people in Junction City. He ruined a lot of people's lives. He's dangerous. Evil. You shouldn't be speaking with him." Michael stammered as he pleaded with Jack.

Jack had had enough fun for the time being. He felt confident and fearless with his newfound talent. "I didn't mean to upset you, Michael. I just thought that you'd be happy that all our time and effort paid off."

Michael simply nodded as he began sweating profusely.

Jack tapped on the counter lightly with his fingers. "Well you have a nice day. I'll be careful, I promise." He turned and left.

"God, help me." Michael slumped into a chair and stared at his trembling hands. He couldn't believe what had just happened. What had he done?

CHAPTER 28

JEFF SAT ON his terrace as he watched little Emily and Sophia play in the sand. His mind rarely played tricks on him anymore. The frequency of visits from angry spirits seemed to have lessened. He couldn't remember the last time he'd been gripped by debilitating fear, nor did he want to remember. Just then, Jeff felt a presence behind him. When he turned his body, Al Martinez appeared out of nowhere. He couldn't believe how quietly the man could move. "God, Al, you scared me half to death."

"You look like you've seen a ghost." Al slapped him on the back.

"It's no wonder you are such an accomplished hunter. You are as quiet as a church mouse and as dangerous as a tiger." Jeff caught his breath.

"Jeff, we've never spoken about your troubled past. I don't wish to pressure you into telling me. But, I can see it in your eyes." Al smiled and gave Jeff a serious look.

Jeff felt uncomfortable. He'd felt so much better lately. Apparently not in Al's eyes. "Al, you know I love you like a father, but . . . " Al stopped him.

"There is no need to explain yourself to me. I can tell that you are a good man. Tonight, I will take you to a Temazcal. There you will be reborn. It will be an opportunity for you to exorcize your demons. A Temazcal, or temazcalli, is made of two words, temas, which means bath, and calli, meaning house. At the time of the conquest by the Spaniards, they were found everywhere throughout southern Mexico. When the Spaniards came, they attempted to wipe out all our Temazcal traditions." He grabbed Jeff's shoulder and squeezed it lightly.

Al continued. "The Temazcal is placed according to the cosmic directions: the fire which heats its stones is placed toward the east where our Father, the sun, the god called 'Tonatiuh' rises; he is the light or masculine element which fertilizes the womb of the mother earth (the chamber of the Temazcal itself), and so life is conceived. The doorway through which the bathers enter and leave is positioned toward the south; "the pathway of the dead," which begins with birth and ends in death, (to the right of the path of Sun). Traditional Mexican healing will bring you back. Just as there is mother and father, sun and earth, hot and cold, so to are we born and, in being born, we begin our path toward death."

Jeff was fascinated with Al's description. He listened intently as Al continued. "When we enter the Temazcal, according to legend, we return once again to our mother's womb. We are presided over by the great goddess, Tonantzin also known as Temazcaltoci, the great mother of both gods and humans. She is our beloved mother, concerned with the health of the children and she receives us into her womb to cure us of physical and spiritual ills. The entrance way is low and small, and through it we enter a small, dark, warm and humid space, cutting off the outside world and giving us a chance to look inside and find ourselves again. When we emerge through the narrow opening, it represents our rebirth from the darkness and silence of the womb. You'll become whole again. The demons of your past will leave you alone."

When Al squeezed Jeff's wrist and spoke of demons, Jeff started to believe what Al had to say. People always spoke of demons they had in their lives such as drug addictions, alcoholism, anger issues or personal disorders, maybe these demons were not just personal problems people carried, but angry spirits who took pleasure in tormenting the living.

Jeff thought of all the sleepless nights he had suffered through and began to wonder if an evening in the Temazcal could help him in healing his past. If anything it would be a bonding moment with his father-in-law. Besides, Jeff could never say no to this intriguing man.

CHAPTER 29

THE MEN STOOD together in a circle around the bonfire. Metal baskets of rocks were placed directly on the coals and in the flames. The drive to this location with Al proved to be an adventure in itself. At times the terrain proved almost too treacherous for their little pickup truck. Jeff felt slightly nervous as he eyed the hut with a clay bowl-shaped floor, no windows and a door you had to crawl to get through.

Jeff had assumed the evening would be a father-son bonding experience. Little did he know that Luis, Armand, Garcia and Jesus were there to accompany him on his quest to exorcize his demons. After they'd carried the rocks into the hut, Al spoke to the men. "It's time. Let us remove our clothing."

"Hang on a second," Jeff thought. "No one said anything about being naked in a hut with a bunch of other men."

"Jeff, you can't be reborn with clothes on." Al read Jeff's thoughts from his face.

Luis smiled and added. "Heff, we are all made the same. There is nothing to be afraid of." With those words of encouragement, Jeff removed his clothing and entered the Temazcal.

The extreme heat and lack of oxygen hit Jeff like a sledgehammer to the chest. His first reaction told him to leave this place and never come back. Jeff heard Al's voice as he spoke in a calm manner. "Jeff, you must have a seat and remain still." Jeff heard the voice and knew it to be Al, but the total darkness gave him another reason to flee. However instead of fleeing, Jeff did as he was told and sat down with his legs crossed and remained still. Although he couldn't see his hand in front of his face, colours began to appear. They swirled in circles and shot out sparks like fireworks.

Suddenly, he appeared; the only demon he'd ever known. Cory stood on the edge of a cliff looking down at what appeared to be a raging forest fire. Cory spoke to him in a calm tone. "My only true friend. How good of you to come in my time of need." Jeff looked down at Cory's outstretched hand. Jeff produced an olive branch and placed it in Cory's hand.

"My instructions are very simple. I must jump into the fire with you to achieve the next level in my afterlife." Cory continued. Jeff simply nodded in agreement. They both stood on the edge of the cliff and counted, three, two, one. They both jumped. Cory jumped straight out and Jeff jumped straight up. The leaves from the olive branch tore through Cory's hand and fluttered like confetti as he fell into the fiery pit. When Jeff landed on the cliff's ledge, he lost his footing and almost fell forward into the flames below. He regained his footing by waving the leafless olive branch wildly to regain his balance. Jeff turned and walked toward the white light.

"You gave us quite a fright in there. How are you feeling?" Jeff woke up on the dewy grass with a flashlight shining in his eyes. Al and Luis were both looking at him with concern on their faces. Jeff told them he felt better than ever. He said he was thirsty and felt ten pounds lighter. Over a few drinks by the fire the men explained how Jeff had screamed uncontrollably, thrashed around the floor and had some form of seizure.

Jeff just laughed it off. He wiped the sweat away from his eyes and explained to everyone that he remembered nothing and felt fine now. In fact he felt better than ever.

The reason for Jeff's new found happiness was the absence of an evil spirit named Glaaj. This spirit had spent months toying with Jeff's tired soul and now Jeff was far too successful and happy for his liking. Glaaj was drawn to another host like a magnet and moved into one of the men more vulnerable and unsuspecting who sat inside the Temazcal with Jeff. The spirits new host continued to breath deeply, completely unsuspecting. Glaaj will turn a once mild mannered man into a hate-filled, revenge seeking, and killing machine.

Jeff accidentally brushed Glaaj's arm as he drank his cerveza, laughed and told the childhood story of accidentally burning down the Bigger Burger restaurant. Glaaj felt repulsion from the touch and wished he could scream. Instead he sat around the fire with his normal facade, while inside his mind there was an inexplicable seed of hatred growing. The demon quickly began devouring all the happiness within him.

CHAPTER 30

ALONG THE ROAD overlooking the Martinez homestead, Sophia and Emily picked flowers. It had become their little ritual to pick flowers for Sunday family dinners. She marveled at how much her life had changed in such a short period of time. Indeed she felt blessed as she watched her daughter stick her cute button nose into the centre of an orchid and smile. They'd had several days of rain and it was nice to be outside. She took no notice of the black SUV as it passed them.

Jeff read the local paper and enjoyed an espresso as the SUV raced up the drive to his beautiful home. He smiled internally as the dust settled around the vehicle. He'd been waiting for this day for the past several weeks. As he watched the same two men approach his home, he waved and greeted them with a smile. If all goes according to plan, today will be the last day he will see these men.

"Señor Gonzola and Señor Calderone, what a pleasant surprise. To what do I owe this special visit today?" Jeff marched out to greet them.

The two men seemed a little suspicious of his overly friendly display. Señor Calderone spoke. "Well it appears the upper management has been digging around in our records and they seem concerned with the Martinez property. Of course, this means that Señor Gonzola and I spent many hours reorganizing the Martinez files to hide this beautiful home."

Jeff's smile broadened. He could smell a strong odour of liquor. "So you need payment for your time?" The two men nodded. "So, I am to pay you for doing your job? Does the government not do this already?"

"Do we have a problem?" Calderone glared at him as he spoke.

"I have no problem at all. You see, when I spoke to Señor Alvarez and explained the situation to him; he was more than helpful and much cheaper I might add. In fact, since he is your superior, I would say that you are the one with the problem, gentlemen. You see, Señor Alvarez wondered aloud to me why he'd not received any payment from the money I've been paying the two of you. He agreed not to speak to you until I'd had the pleasure of telling you the good news myself. In person." Jeff laughed.

"It would seem that you have made a dangerous play, Señor." Señor Calderone smiled. The two men looked ready to explode. Jeff simply stood there confidently. He knew how to handle himself and saw all the cards on the table.

"No Señor. You were warned not to go to the well too often. I'll be sure to tell the good news to Alverez about our latest visit. I'm sure that he will be pleased to hear that you were prepared to keep more bribes in only your pockets. Now get in your vehicle and go straight to hell." Jeff smiled in triumph.

The men got back in the SUV with tinted windows

and sprayed sand and tiny stones into the air as they raced off. As they approached the blind curve ahead, their extra speed and wet road conditions caused the vehicle to drift. Calderone gave a little more gas as the vehicle fishtailed around the corner much like a rally racecar.

This time, Sophia did take notice of the SUV as it gunned its engine. She screamed and clutched her little Emily in her arms. The rear quarter panel hit them with a sickening crunch and threw them beyond the flowers they'd been picking.

The SUV never stopped to see if the woman and child were okay. Later, some would speculate that they might not have seen the two crouched by the side of the road.

Jeff heard the screams in the distance, as did a few others. However, when he heard them, he felt some sort of connection inside himself break. It felt like several piano wires being cut at once. He ran like a man possessed.

CHAPTER 31

THEY BOUNCED IN the back of the pick up truck while Al maneuvered as quickly as humanly possible to the medical clinic. Sophia clutched little Emily in her arms as Jeff held them both tightly. The scene would have been very romantic if not for the tragic circumstances. Little Emily would have loved a ride in Granddad's truck. The child's skin had turned blue as Sophia held her. At the scene, no one had tried to remove the child from Sophia's arms. There appeared to be major trauma to the toddler's skull. As for Sophia, she drifted in and out of consciousness.

"Jeff, I'm not going to make it. I'm dying. I feel so stupid that I haven't told you yet that I am pregnant. I didn't want to tell you because of all the jellyfish this time of year. And you know how I hate jellyfish." Her last few rambling words were slurred.

Jeff kissed her bloody forehead. "Please, Sophia hold on. We're almost there." he begged her. The sun was setting as they neared the clinic. As the vehicle passed homes, people already knew of the tragedy. Word of the accident had spread at an alarming rate. The town's little angel had been injured.

The medical clinic was run by the Mexican branch of the Red Cross in a minimalist small brick building with a beige aluminum roof. The doors and windows were filthy from the dust created by vehicles as they drove on the dirt roads. Jeff hoisted Sophia out of the vehicle and carried everything that mattered to him into the clinic. Al's eyes were wet with tears as he held the door open for them. A French nurse with short dark hair and lean features quickly escorted them to a back room with metal cabinetwork. He laid Sophia on the cot in the centre of the white room. The doctor checked Sophia's vital signs as Jeff crouched next to him. He was an American volunteering his skills, trying to make a difference. He had a round face with a pasty complexion and wore thick glasses. Jeff's insides were in turmoil, worse than anything he'd experienced in the past, this was worse than losing his mother, his fiancé, his best friend or his previous life. He struggled to keep from retching as his world crumbled around him.

Tears rolled down his cheeks as the doctor spoke very slowly to him. "I'm Dr. Wolfe. Your wife is bleeding internally. It's a miracle she is still alive. We must remove your daughter from her arms so that I can get her some fluids. The nurse will draw blood from her father. I don't want to risk moving her again. I'll have to do the operation here. We must stop the bleeding."

Jeff could only nod to the man in the white coat. He followed Dr. Wolfe's instructions. He whispered in Sophia's ear. "Honey, I am going to take Emily over to the other side of the room. Please let go dear." She released her daughter to her husband's arms. Jeff squeezed his little Emily's lifeless body and suppressed a mournful cry. With tears flowing freely, he passed her body to the nurse.

Again, Dr. Wolfe addressed Jeff. "I must stress to you that we are not a hospital. We are only a clinic equipped for minor surgeries. If we move your wife to Vera Cruz, she will surely die. I'm telling you this to prepare you for the worst."

Jeff sat in the waiting area and filled out paperwork for Emily's death with Al's help. His emotional state was quickly deteriorating. Inside this run-down clinic in Zempoala, his wife lay fighting for her life. "How could this be happening?" he thought.

Dr. Wolfe met with them several hours later and said, "Your wife is in critical condition. I was able to stop the bleeding from the lacerations on her liver and spleen, but she is going to need more blood. We need to leave her here overnight in hopes that she stabilizes enough for us to move her to the Hospital of Maria in Vera Cruz. You gentlemen are welcome to stay here overnight. I am sorry for your loss."

Dr. Wolfe paused and spoke quietly to the nurse. "There is still the matter of the death certificate that was filed earlier for the daughter Emily. Don't forget there is a charge for the government paperwork of forty-five American dollars. If they cannot afford to pay this, little Emily's death will go unrecorded, like so many others here in the village." On that cold note the doctor walked away.

Jeff sat motionless with his bloody hands on his face as he thought of Emily's lifeless body. He turned to Al who embraced him as he cried uncontrollably.

CHAPTER 32

S EVERAL HOURS LATER, La Policia arrived in front of the Red Cross clinic in an older white vehicle, with a blue stripe and matching lights. An officer stepped out of the vehicle. Between the great effort it took him to get out of his car and his far too tight stretching uniform, it was evident that this cop spent more time sitting behind a desk than chasing criminals. The officer's loose inner tube like belly jiggled as he struggled to get up the stairs. He meandered in to speak with Jeff and Al about the accident.

He spoke in static bursts of Spanish as he directed his large bumpy liver-spotted nose in Jeff's direction. Al did his best to calm Jeff down as he grew more and more frustrated with the officer's questions. "Did you see the vehicle that hit your wife and daughter? Are you certain there was no other vehicle on the road? What makes you think this black S.U.V. struck them? What makes you think this was intentional and not an accident?" Jeff lost his patience, slammed his fist in disgust against the wall behind the annoying officer and went to Sophia's bedside. Al apologized profusely for his son-in-law's outburst.

As he knelt beside her, he was overwhelmed with

pain and grief. His vision blurred from heavy tears. He grabbed hold of her hand and felt the coolness of her skin. As he wiped his eyes, he began to take notice of her skin colour. It looked grey and ashen. Quickly, he scrambled to his feet and shouted for the nurse.

The nurse sprung into action, checking her blood pressure and pulse. Her body language told a story of a nurse who was frustrated with the lack of proper equipment and medication. She grabbed a penlight and scanned Sophia's pupils, looking for a sign that the brain was functioning. The nurse shook her head from side to side. "We must send for Dr. Wolfe!" Dr. Wolfe had left moments earlier for supper.

Seconds later, the wooden cot groaned and creaked as Sophia's body began to convulse. Jeff began to scream, "No, no, no." in a panic as he pleaded for the nurse to do something to help his wife. Suddenly, she was still. His confused screams of panic turned to screams of grief as the nurse moved him out of the way and checked for vital signs. Finding none, the nurse began C.P.R. procedures. After an exhaustive attempt to revive Sophia the nurse covered her dead body with a bed sheet. Al and the officer came into the clinic and helped escort him out of the room. Jeff bolted from Al and the officer's grasp and ran out of the clinic repeatedly yelling, "Emily! Sophia! No, no!"

CHAPTER 33

THE BELL ON the Tattoo You's front door tinkled as Michael opened up the shop and turned on the lights. He scanned the signs along the walls and examined some of the tired posters that needed updating. The youth of today were starting to take interest in anime. Maybe a new section on anime would drum up some clientele. Living at Jeff's place had really improved his outlook on life and given him more direction.

The door opened and Michael's blood ran cold as Jack stood in front of his counter without saying a word. He wore no shoes, blue jeans, and a white shirt and suit jacket. Michael spoke hesitantly to his deranged-looking former customer.

"Jack, how are you?" Michael asked.

Still, Jack said nothing.

"Jack you are looking kind of pale. Can I get you a glass of water or something?" Michael persisted.

Jack slowly came out of a trance-like state. "We've been doing quite a bit of automatic writing these days. I'm not sure I've slept this week."

"What is automatic writing?" Michael expressed his confusion.

"As a medium, I allow Cory to control my hand and write out messages. He's been very thought provoking. His descriptions of the great beyond have been gripping to say the least. I've come to give you this." Jack confirmed Michael's worst fears.

In slow motion, Jack reached inside his jacket. Instinctively Michael dove his large body behind the counter and waited for the hail of bullets that would end his life. Calmly, Jack walked around to the back of the counter and looked down. In his hand he held a rolled up sheet of paper tied with a blood red ribbon.

Oh God, thought Michael. He whipped the paper out of Jack's hand, picked himself off the dusty floor and said. "Don't ever come here again. I mean it. If you so much as show up on the sidewalk, the cops will be here to take you away. I warned you to stay away from Cory. Look at you! You're a disaster. Get out. Get out now!" Michael's fear practically overwhelmed him.

In a zombie-like trance, Jack Armstrong and his Ouija board tattoo exited the building. Michael ran to the door and locked it. His brow dripped with sweat from the exertion. He stared at the rolled up sheet of paper. Every instinct told him to strike a match and light this message ablaze. He sat down in a chair and slowly unrolled the paper.

The message contained complex caricatures depicting the Junction City Four. The sketch included details only known by Cory. Written over and over on the page were the same words: 'Michael come to me. We were meant to stay together as a group. Bring Jeff. Michael come to me.'

The words repeated endlessly on the page with the writing growing smaller and smaller. Michael remembered how Cory used to write this way as a joke. He would usually hand a large piece of paper to someone to read. As they would get to the small print they would hold the paper closer to their face to read; at which point Cory would smack the paper into the persons nose. It would keep the group laughing for hours. Except for the person with the bloody nose. The more pain Cory could cause the more they would laugh.

Michael was not laughing now, he was more frightened than ever.

CHAPTER 34

I N A COMPLETELY deranged state, Jeff arrived late in the evening at his home, a bloody mess. His clothes were torn from running into objects and madly continuing to run into the night. He ran into his home and searched for something to control the storm that raged inside him. In the liquor cabinet he found half a bottle of Tequila and drank it in three large gulps. It burned his throat and stomach. He fought his body's desire to bring the harsh liquor back up. Next he found a three-quarter full bottle of Crown Royal and drank greedily from it.

The alcohol began to take effect as he sat in his leather chair. When he attempted to stand, his vision blurred and his balance left him. He fell and landed flat on his face on the wood floor. The crushing emotional pain had left his chest and was replaced with total darkness.

When Jeff regained consciousness he looked over at all of the photos of Emily and remembered joyous times. From the floor he could almost hear her giggles filling the house. His thoughts then turned to his beloved Sophia and how her warm affection had healed his damaged soul. Jeff screamed out loud. "God, why is this happening to me?" His tormented screams blotted out the memories of giggles and love. He knew what must be done.

Jeff scrambled to his feet and left through the back door to search in the rear of the yard. He found what he was looking for located next to the water storage tanks near the generator. He marched unsteadily over to the beach with the answer to his problems in each hand. In this very spot the family would celebrate and gather to have bonfires. He sucked in a large breath of fresh air and tears rolled down his face. Filled with despair, he raised the first container of gasoline above his head and poured the liquid over his body. The gas seeped into the tiny cuts and abrasions on his body and sent a cold pain to his temples. He welcomed the pain. He knew there would be more to come. As he grabbed the next container to dump over himself, he fell over and landed head first into the sand. He cursed himself for being so clumsy. With a face full of wet sand, he got back to his feet. Again, the gasoline trickling down his body gave a cold burn when it came into contact with his skin.

Jeff's hands trembled as he dug into his pocket for his gold Zippo lighter. He pulled it out and without hesitation began working the knurled wheel, but his hands were wet and his thumb kept slipping. The smell of the fuel made his head spin, or maybe it was the copious amounts of alcohol he'd consumed. He attempted to dry his thumb on his gasoline-soaked shirt to get better traction on the little wheel. At that moment he thought he heard a voice in the distance. It didn't matter. He finally got a spark, then a flame and then a raging inferno as burning vapours engulfed him.

CHAPTER 35

THE SUN HAD set and the evening light had dissipated. Al Martinez consoled his grieving wife as he held her in his arms. The entire family sat in shock. Indeed this was the saddest day in the history of the Martinez family.

"Get your mother some water please. She has been crying for hours now." Al commanded Garcia. When Garcia came back with the water, Maria refused to drink it.

Jesus noticed lights over at Sophia's house. He felt a pang as he realized it was the house where Sophia and Emily used to live. He spoke to his father. "Looks like Jeff is back."

"You must go get him and bring him here. He should not be alone at a time like this. He is family. Go quickly." Al's face showed concern and fear.

Jesus didn't understand why, but for the first time in his life his father's words carried immense urgency. Jesus flew out the front door and ran in a full sprint toward the house. The lights inside the home were like a beacon as he maneuvered over shrubs in the sand. Seconds before he reached the front porch his attention was drawn toward the ocean and he spotted Jeff. His mind quickly processed the information before his eyes. Jesus yelled out to him. "Jeff, stop! Stop right now!" He sprinted toward his gasoline-soaked brother-in-law. Twenty feet before he reached him, Jeff burst into flames.

Without hesitation Jesus lunged at him with the power of a linebacker and wrapped his arms around his waist. The intense heat burnt his hair and arms as he pushed him into the water. Jesus rolled with him in the water along the sandy shore. The flames glowed beneath the water's surface as they extinguished. Jesus couldn't believe what had just happened. He looked down at Jeff and noticed that he wasn't moving.

"Jeff, Jeff! Damn you, don't die!" Jesus slapped him hard across the face while cursing in Spanish. Over the years he'd grown to like his intriguing American brother-in-law. His easy-going lifestyle, hearty laugh and thousand-watt smile were infectious.

The flames, along with the shouting and screaming, alerted Al and Garcia. The men came running over the sand dunes in the moonlight. They abandoned caution as they raced to help save Jeff from himself. When they arrived on the beach, they discovered Jesus dragging an unconscious Jeff out of the water. Together the men picked him up like a wounded soldier and rushed him into his home.

In the warm interior of the beautiful mahogany living room, the three men inspected the damage to Jeff's body as they placed him on the leather sofa. They were alarmed to see his clothing was practically all burnt away. Even more disturbing was the fact that he remained unconscious as if in a coma. There had been so much tragedy in such a short time. The Martinez men felt devastated and helpless.

CHAPTER 36

FOR SIX DAYS Jeff laid in the master bedroom on the king size mattress in a catatonic state. The room should have been a testament to love and family. But instead, the room was a prison for a man whose life had been torn apart. The Martinez family stood around the bed as Dr. Wolfe examined him.

The same doctor who had failed to save his wife stood over Jeff with a penlight in his right hand. Dr. Wolfe swiped the light back and forth to observe his patient's pupils. Next he grasped the right arm and raised it to a forty-five-degree angle. The arm remained in position, motionless, seemingly frozen. The doctor demonstrated the effects of catatonia by pushing down on the upraised arm. The arm would not budge. He then pulled out a needle from his bag and inserted it into Jeff's left heel. Nothing happened.

Dr. Wolfe spoke to the family slowly and with purpose. "This is worse than I feared. Luckily, the burns are superficial. Maria, I must say that you would have made a fine nurse. You've used the gauze and ointments exactly as prescribed. Unfortunately, at issue is this state of catatonia Jeff appears to be in. The correct term for this condition is called a "stupor": a motionless state where the patient doesn't react to external stimuli. Individuals in this state make little-to-no eye contact and in this case, remain mute and rigid. As you can see, his arm remains in the upright position." Dr. Wolfe motioned toward Jeff.

Al looked over at his two sons and wife. He spoke with concern in his heart. "Dr. Wolfe, what can be done? We've already lost so much. We need some sort of balance amidst all this sadness." Earlier in the day, Sophia and Emily had been buried on the hill overlooking the village. Every woman in attendance had beaten the ground with her fists as she screamed in pain at the injustice of the deaths.

Dr. Wolfe continued. "I know, Señor Martinez. You must trust that we are doing everything we can. This tragedy has shaken me, as well as the entire village. The problem is that we are waiting for benzodiazepine and lorazepam. Those medications should cure Mr. Brooks of his catatonia. For now you will have to have someone stay with him. You must prepare yourself for the possibility that he may not come out of this state."

Dr. Wolfe packed his bags and on his way out praised Maria once again on her fine work. The Martinez family entered the living room to give the bad news to all the extended family that had stayed after the funeral to give their condolences to Jeff.

Luis held his wife in his arms, his damaged hand a reminder of his stupidity while building the home he now sat in. What a beautiful home he'd built. Such tragedy, he thought to himself. His rambunctious boys had been sent outside in the cool night air to burn off energy. The last thing the situation needed was yelling. Armand and his family were in attendance, as was most of Maria's side of the family, many of whom also had a hand in building the home. Luis spoke as the Martinez family came down the stairs. "How is Heff? Tell me he is going to be okay."

There had been growing concern for the Martinez family in the community. When relatives had pleaded with Al to let them come and help, he had turned them away and asked for time for his family to grieve in peace. They had become almost like celebrities in their tiny community of family and friends.

Al addressed the large group he had invited and gave everyone the sad news about Jeff. He told them of his recovering burns. He commended Jesus for his heroics in saving Jeff from certain death. Lastly, he told them of Jeff's catatonic state and how the doctor had explained that the family should prepare for the worst. Everyone sat down in stunned silence.

Everyone felt sad except for one man. Ever since the evening in the Temazcal, Glaaj's anger seemed to have no purpose or direction. Now, as he sat in the living room and planned for his first release of anger, his excitement grew.

CHAPTER 37

LAAJ SAT OUTSIDE the modest Gonzola home, located in the heart of Vera Cruz. He was shielded from prying eyes by bushes beneath the window. The blackness in his heart increased as he listened to the heated conversation between the extortionist and his fiery Latin wife. He watched the washing sway on the clothesline in the backyard. In this heat, the clothes would be dry in no time at all.

"I'll find another job. You make it sound like our life is over." Gonzola spoke to his wife with contempt in his voice. He paused as a hateful comment crossed his mind. "Funny how it seems that the only time you seem to grow a spine and stand up to me is when it's that time of the month. Which means, of course, once again you are not pregnant! An infertile woman! Why do I stay with you?" Glaaj observed as the neighbour's lights came on and a few faces looked in the direction of the screaming.

Glaaj flinched at the sound of shattering glass. The wife now spewed her own string of venomous retorts. "You stay with me because my family owns this house, you're a worthless excuse for a man. If my womb is barren, it is because your pencil has no lead. Or maybe it is because you'll sleep with whichever whore opens her legs. You lost your job because you followed that idiot Calderone like a little puppy. Why do I stay with you, is the real question. All you two morons had to do was ask for cash from unsuspecting peasants. Why don't you go to the pub and see what sort of smelly whore you can find tonight? You'll need a bed! Get out of my house!"

Glaaj heard a scuffle and a slap, followed by passionate grunts and groans. Those two deserve each other, he thought. Glaaj seized the opportunity to grab what he'd come for. He removed a pair of pants and a shirt from the washing line. He stuffed them into his bag under the cover of darkness. Just as he finished there was more screaming from inside the home. "Get out you bastard. You still need a place to sleep tonight." The front door burst open as Gonzola shot out. Glaaj didn't need to follow him. He would be easy to find, Pub Armadillo was downhill from his home.

Battle plans were being set into motion more quickly than Glaaj had expected. That suited him just fine. His mind found time to wonder about the different reasons the world had gone to war. His favourite was the story of the Iraqi conflict. In the 1990's, Saddam Hussein invaded Kuwait over an insult to all Iraqi women. The Iraqi foreign minister was told by the Emir of Kuwait that sanctions against Iraq would not stop until every Iraqi woman was turned into a ten-dollar prostitute.

Glaaj forced himself to return to his mission. He would only be victorious in this conflict if he kept his eye on capturing the man who had a hand in the death of Emily and Sophia. This felt just like a war to him. He felt more prepared than ever. Every war had its casualties.

Millions of people died every day for no apparent reason. For him, the death of Emily and Sophia was reason enough to go to war.

This man Gonzola would die because he had a hand in killing Sophia and Emily Martinez. Gonzola's wife would die just to cause him pain.

CHAPTER 38

Gonzola sat on the bar stool feeling sorry for himself. How could his life have deteriorated so quickly? The last several hours he'd spent drinking weren't solving his problems. The bar stool next to him scraped the old wooden floor as Glaaj sat next to his drunken target. The two men drank in silence as they listened to a soccer match on the radio.

"Some weather we're having. But it looks like you have more on your mind than just the weather." (Glaaj broke the ice.) But, Gonzola didn't take the bait. He kept staring at the liquor bottles lined up behind the bar.

Glaaj tried a more direct approach. "My name is Peter. I'm your new neighbour four houses down."

"Welcome to the neighbourhood. Do yourself a favour and don't talk to me. All my bad luck may rub off on you." Gonzola turned to get a better look at Glaaj. "Hey, you do look sort of familiar. Have we met before?"

Glaaj simply shook his head. "Maybe from around the neighbourhood." Gonzola may have had a better chance in recognizing Glaaj if he had not been wearing a ball cap and glasses.

As the night wore on and Gonzola's empty glasses piled up along the bar, Glaaj found his new friend becoming more talkative. He almost felt sorry for his victim, but his level of contempt far outweighed his pity. Finally, Glaaj said what he had rehearsed earlier, "My wife sent me over here to make sure things were all right. She thought it would be the nice, neighbourly thing to do. We couldn't help overhearing you and your wife's argument. When I was walking over here, your wife was out in your front yard. I asked her if she was okay. She seemed really drunk and I tried to convince her to go back into her house and sleep it off. That's when she invited me in. She pulled at my clothes and said she could really show me a good time."

"That bitch. She's doing it just to get back at me. Wait until I get my hands on her!" Gonzola flew into a rage, knocking over his stool as he stood and screamed.

"Perfect," thought Glaaj, as he stared in the direction of the little old bartender. The old man could recite word for word the theatrics he'd just witnessed.

"Hold on there partner." With a bear-like grip, Glaaj forced Gonzola back to his barstool. Gonzola seemed to be emotionally drained and quickly relaxed. Glaaj continued, "I told you about your wife so you wouldn't be surprised at her drunken state."

Glaaj bought him the biggest beer on tap. "She also told me that if I were to see you, I should send you home this evening. She said something about wanting the fighting to end. She was crying." Glaaj whispered those words out of earshot of the bartender. Feeling confident that his plan had worked, he paid the tab and wished his new friend luck.

Glaaj noticed that the Vera Cruz air had turned chilly as he raced uphill back to the Gonzola home. The cool air helped him mentally prepare for phase two of the operation. Glaaj changed at the side of the house into the clothes he'd taken earlier. The pants were shorter than his own, a little looser, and the shirt too tight. No matter. He wouldn't be wearing them for long.

There were no lights or sounds coming from the house as he entered through the unlocked front door. He quickly made his way to the kitchen and silently grabbed a large kitchen knife. Now it was time to find his target. He went from one small room to another in the three-bedroom home. He finally found her in the living area, sleeping on the sofa. Glaaj and his host together saw the purpose of their mission lying in front of them. Although his host had slaughtered many animals on the farm, this would certainly be different. Glaaj filled with rage and steeled his host's nerves as they prepared to kill their first human being.

The flashes of the knife were quick and precise. He wasted no time since he was unsure as to how much time he had. She rolled around and flopped, but there was very little resistance. She never had time to cry out in pain since her vocal chords had been cut cleanly through. Glaaj went into a rhythm as he slashed his victim repeatedly. Blood sprayed on the walls and the furniture.

Glaaj wondered how long Gonzola would take to finish his beer, or even if he might order another one or two more beers. The wait would surely be worth it. He lit several candles to make a path from the front door to the living room.

The evil inside him doubled in size as he sat and waited.

CHAPTER 39

G ONZOLA ARRIVED HOME and stumbled up the first few steps. He turned to examine the stairs; he gave them the same accusing look a baseball player gives his glove after he mishandles the ball. Seeing nothing wrong with the stairs, he opened the front door. The alcohol in his system gave him a feeling of peace and acceptance toward his plight. Once inside, he noticed the glow of the candles in the darkened home.

As Gonzola followed the lit path, he wondered what could have turned his wife's mood so quickly. Normally, the home would have remained in a storm-watch for days after this evening's events. Gonzola never expected to feel the cold steel of a blade enter his abdomen. He looked down. Protruding from his stomach was the black handle of his kitchen knife. Only once lying on the floor did he look up and take notice of his blood-soaked attacker. The pain intensified as Glaaj gripped the knife firmly and gave it a slight wiggle to get his victim's attention. Gonzola grabbed for his attacker's arms, but his hands slipped on the slick blood. This provided the perfect transfer of evidence. Gonzola's hands were now covered in his wife's blood.

Glaaj spoke softly to him. "Your wife is over on the sofa resting comfortably. Well, not so much resting. More like bleeding out. Now that I have you in a position to talk, I thought I would clarify all the questions I'm certain are floating in your head. Firstly, I'm here as a favour to the Martinez family. You were extorting money from them over the summer. You and Calderone killed Sophia and Emily with your black SUV. Did you know about that?" Glaaj wiggled the knife and the scream almost shattered glass. Gonzola shook his head and begged for mercy. Glaaj pretended not to hear the answer to his rhetorical question. "Do you notice my fine apparel? You should. They're your clothes covered in your wife's blood. Once your heart stops beating, I'll put them on you. It will be another sad lover's quarrel gone wrong."

When he spoke those final words, the angry fire within him exploded. He turned the blade upwards and forced it up through the muscle tissue, only the breastbone forced him to stop. It proved to be considerably more resistant than he'd imagined. Gonzola expired quickly and the stage was set perfectly. The already troubled Gonzola marriage tragically ended when the husband slaughtered his wife and then committed hara-kiri (made famous by Japanese samurai). Quickly, he removed the slippery, blood soaked clothes and then pulled the knife from Gonzola. He then re-dressed Gonzola. He paid close attention to properly buttoning the shirt and pants on the victim. Lastly, he cut the shirt material in the same manner of the wound on the body and reinserted the knife into Gonzola. He stood back and admired his work. He thought of one more detail: from the kitchen he got an empty margarine container and collected blood from the woman on the couch. He then flicked it with his fingers onto Gonzola's face. The scene was now set and the performance concluded.

Glaaj left out the back door using plastic bags over his hand to conceal his prints on the door handles. He changed into his previous evening's clothes after hosing himself off in the backyard under the cover of darkness. He welcomed the feeling of cool water on his skin. His temples pulsed with every beat of his heart. The thrill of finally having a purpose for his anger proved almost overwhelming. Under the starlit Vera Cruz sky, Glaaj melted into the darkness.

CHAPTER 40

JACK ARMSTRONG STOOD in the dense forest of Junction City's outskirts, following a hand drawn map. The cool air plumed around him like smoke. A couple of miles south of South Park, he encountered a large flat rock. Certainly, Armstrong never imagined the trouble he'd create when he got a large Ouija board tattoo on his back. His overindulgence of his obsession with the afterlife had led his own life out of control. The hand drawn map was the result of another free writing episode with the spirit.

Next to the large flat rock surrounded by trees, tucked into a crevice, he found three journals in a plastic bag. After placing the journals in his pack, Jack examined his surroundings and he could feel the enormous spiritual presence in this place. When he stumbled and fell into the dirt, he figured it was from lack of sleep. Every hour something in his room would slide across the floor or fall from a shelf. It had gotten to the point where he slept more at work than he did at home.

His mind raced with the excitement of being in the exact same area as the spirit. Still on the ground, he examined what he first thought was dirt. In fact, mixed in with the leaves were hundreds of small bones. From Cory's description, this was definitely the place. After dusting himself off, he proceeded with the task at hand. The plastic bag made a rustling noise as he removed it from the pack. Old Mrs. Oberon's lapdog, Fluffy, lay dead inside the bag. Armstrong surmised the lapdog had been another reason for his lack of sleep. A quick jerk on the animal's neck (after finding it in the hallway) snapped its spine and ended the incessant whining and yapping from next-door forever.

The dead lapdog lay on its back ready for the procedure. Although he had never done anything like this in his entire life, Armstrong felt prepared for the task at hand. He wasted no time with his first incision from above the anus to the breastplate. There he examined the organs, stomach content, heart, liver, lungs and intestines. He found a few lesions that he assumed to be cancerous. Maybe he did the old girl a favour. After washing his hands in a very cold stream nearby, he proceeded to add to the half-full journal he'd found in the plastic bag. After entering all the medical information, he received a freehand message from Cory. "Good job. Treat yourself! Get some surgical tools!"

CHAPTER 41

WHILE GLAAJ PLANNED for his next mission, safely tucked away in his farm community, Calderone was told the news of his former partner over the phone. He stood in his kitchen with the phone to his ear, frowning in disbelief. How could a man he'd known for so long take his own life and that of his wife? He'd always known that Gonzola's wife was a temperamental woman who didn't put up with any of his crap. The fact that he snapped and killed her was shocking, but not exactly unexpected. But, to take his life afterwards seemed out of character? Calderone wasn't convinced.

People who lived next to killers often say, 'They were nice quiet neighbour's'. In this case, the neighbour's were saying just the opposite to the media. "The Gonzola's fought constantly. It wasn't uncommon to see lamps and suitcases flying out the windows. The night of the murder, shouts and screams were heard in the evening heat. The bartender at Pub Armadillo overheard Gonzola threaten his wife during a heated conversation that evening. The question remains, could this tragedy have been prevented?" The police who investigated the death were simply going through the motions. After conducting interviews and reviewing the overwhelming blood evidence, the case was deemed a murder/suicide.

Calderone didn't spend too much time grieving over the loss of his former partner, as he and Gonzola never really had any connection. They were two very different men. Over the years he'd enjoyed dabbling in real estate and investments. All the wealthy people Calderone had met owned real estate. In fact, he'd made several friends in the business and tried to help Gonzola with his money issues. But Gonzola wanted to hear none of it. Calderone planned to use his rugged good looks and charm as a tool in his next career choice of real-estate salesman. He was actually glad to say good-bye to his old career. After so many years working for the government of Mexico, it was time for a change. All the corruption made him feel dirty.

Calderone and his family were planning a trip to a small cabin next to the Gulf Coast. Some family time seemed to be just what the doctor ordered. Financially, he'd done well for himself. The money he'd made/extorted over the years was spent on real estate and investments; unlike Gonzola, who had spent his money on his girlfriends, booze and gambling. Calderone's life, as well as his marriage to Veronica, made others jealous. Together with a seven-year-old son, Jacob, and a nine-year-old daughter, Anna, they were the picture of success and happiness.

"Dad what is that on the car?" Calderone's son helped his father carry the bags to the car. He stopped and pointed to the windshield.

Calderone removed a plain white paper from the wiper blade. The message was written in brown ink, or so he thought. He made no connection between the murders and the very simple note.

The first thing that came to mind was the day Alverez fired them. That bastard took great pleasure in mocking them before he kicked them out of his office. "Outsmarted by peasants? Not exactly the sharpest pencils in the box are you?"

Gonzola (God rest his soul) never backed down from a fight and only made matters worse. "He wasn't a peasant, he was an American, and besides the only reason you are the boss is because of your ability to kiss ass!"

Alverez gave them both a death stare as his face turned red. "At least I know when to keep my mouth shut. You're both fired. Leave your things and get out.

Calderone forgot about the past and looked at his son as he read the note one more time. "Minus two. Doesn't make sense to me."

Chapter 42

GLAAJ PASSED THE Calderone home for the second time that day. All signs pointed to the family having gone on an extended trip. He parked his rusting Toyota pick-up truck two blocks over and made his way to the home. The ocean spray rusts vehicles just as quickly as road salt in winter climates and his truck was a testament of the damaging sea salt air.

Compared with the Gonzolas, the Calderones lived in a much nicer two-storey home. He gained back door access with relative ease, by manipulating the tumblers with a small pick and turning the handle. Once inside the home, he studied every detail he could about the family. He made notes on Jacob and Anna, how many awards they'd won. He found Veronica's diary and took notes on every personal detail. The family's telephone directory proved to be the biggest jackpot, he wrote out the entire Calderone family tree and gained valuable financial information. Glaaj took careful steps not to disturb anything he touched. Every paper was replaced in its original position.

Glaaj made himself at home, reading over his notes at the maple kitchen table. He leapt up and headed for the refrigerator. The family cat swirled around his legs while he examined the contents. He considered pulling out his knife; slaughtering the animal and using the carcass as a bloody sponge to write a large number three on the kitchen wall. Maybe that would trigger the right response. Clearly, his note had proved to be too vague. He knew better though, this mission was strictly for information. The milk and yogurt would expire in another week. Therefore, he surmised, the family would return in the next day or two. But he needed to make sure.

He picked up the phone, examined the time, 9:50 p.m., and dialed the number he'd already committed to memory. "Hola, Señora Calderone. Sorry for calling so late. My name is Peter Farrah with the Union Fenosa power electric company. We are investing six hundred million American dollars into the Tuxpan plants, creating more than 983 megawatts of power. The two plants are almost ready. I've been trying to contact your son for the last several days. He gave me your number in case of an emergency. You see, we're about to close a major land deal and we could use him as a real-estate agent to speak with the people in the surrounding areas. Do you know how I could get in touch with him?" He took notes and listened intently as the old woman described in detail where her son could be found. Also, when he would return.

"Thank you Señora Calderone. You've been very helpful. Tell me would you be interested in free electricity? You see the Union Fenosa Company requires a certain number of test subjects and since your son and I will be doing business together and you've been so helpful, why shouldn't you benefit as well." He listened to the old woman as she excitedly gave directions to her home. "Excellent, just a few more questions. How many appliances are in the home? What kind of bathtub do you own? Is the hot water heated with electricity?" On a pad he jotted down the information. "Well, thank you very much. This will allow me to get a jump-start on the paper work. See you tomorrow morning. Good night."

Chapter 43

IN THE EARLY dawn, Al Martinez grabbed a hold of a sow's ears as he guided the pig into a separate pen for birth. He'd learned some valuable lessons hunting with his father when it came to pigs. A pig's bite is more powerful than that of a large dog, and once an animal has a taste for blood it will devour an entire carcass, including the bones.

Jesus was working hard tagging and sorting the animals in the adjacent barn when Garcia walked in. Jesus stopped and looked at him in surprise. "You look like hell. Where have you been? Dad has been wondering about where you have been these past few days."

Garcia took his time answering. "I took a trip up to the hills to do a little hunting. I needed some time to sort things out. How do you manage to deal with everything so easily?"

"I work. I do what needs doing. A man can run and hide when he faces adversity or he can stand and fight. I am choosing to stand and fight." Jesus wasn't expecting a heart-to-heart with his twin brother.

"You trying to say that I turned and ran? You looking for a fight?" Garcia looked at his brother.

Jesus laughed. "You always think I'm attacking you. There is nothing wrong with going into the woods and finding a solution to your problems. If the problem takes over your life that is when you need to rethink what needs to be done."

"How have Mom and Dad been?" Garcia said as he stared into the distance thoughtfully.

"Mom has been crying herself to sleep every night. She is still taking regular shifts caring for Jeff. We all are. Right now Luis is taking a shift. At least Jeff is eating these days. He still hasn't said a word though. You want to go over and see him? Might do you some good and I could use a break." Jesus sighed.

They walked over to the house in silence. The death of Sophia still carried a heavy sting for the Martinez family. Both men kept their emotions in check as they walked slowly to the steps. When they crossed the grand entrance, they spotted Luis sleeping on the couch, snoring loudly. They didn't disturb his slumber; instead they quietly marched up the steps to the master bedroom.

Jeff lay on his side as the two entered the room. They were alarmed to see all the dried blood as they walked up to Jeff lying on his bed. What had happened? Quickly, the two checked for any wounds. Seeing nothing wrong, they began to clean his face, neck and hands with soap and water. Gently they reapplied the burn cream left by the doctor. As usual, Jeff took no notice of them.

In regards to his burns, Jeff had been incredibly lucky. His main injuries were to his legs, shoulders and a small patch on his forehead. Clothing and a hat could eventually cover them all. If only his emotional scars would heal so easily.

Jesus spoke to Garcia in a hush. "We've got to tell someone about all this blood. I mean I don't get it. Is it from his wounds drying and then cracking? We should tell this to Dr. Wolfe and ask him if this is normal."

Garcia broke in. "No! I don't think this was his blood. We've got to speak to Luis and find out if he heard Jeff leave. The doctor said there was a chance of him sleep walking."

"So what, he went out and killed something?" Jesus looked baffled.

"Or someone!" Garcia looked at his twin gravely.

CHAPTER 44

G LAAJ STOOD IN front of the animals on his father's farm, marking the pigs destined for slaughter with an X. He relived the success of his plot against the government workers. His anger, which had seemed so pointless in the past, now had a true purpose. In times of war, soldiers' lives were sacrificed for a mere parcel of land. It was this line of thinking which allowed him to flourish and embrace his mission.

Once he finished the morning chores, Glaaj packed his cooler with a lunch consisting of wild boar on a bun, yogurt and a grape soda for later. After the drive from Zempoala to Vera Cruz, his little pick-up truck welcomed the break from the switchbacks and hills along the coast. The truck slowed to a stop on the open, flat street as he double-checked the address of Camilla Calderone's small single family home. The house's orange canopies covering the windows, and the red and yellow trim, gave the old home a gingerbread house look. As he walked up the cobblestone walkway he thought to himself, 'Big candy canes would finish this nicely'. He put on a large friendly smile.

The pastel green door opened with a creak. Camilla

gave the toothy grin of a lonely woman and greeted the sharply dressed man with an exuberant "Hola." She was a tall woman for her age whose posture seemed to have straightened with time. The home's decor matched the exterior. Glaaj felt a sudden urge to place his sunglasses on or start painting everything white. He closed his eyes, took a deep breath and pulled out his official looking clipboard.

He smiled back, equally pleased to see the old woman alone. "Señora Calderone, how good to finally meet you. You're looking very youthful today. What is your secret?" He paid no attention to her answer. A pawn serves no purpose, he reminded himself. After rambling through questions that sounded very official, he now asked her for directions. "I'll need you to fill your tub with hot-water while I test the voltage intake of your hot-water tank. Could you show me to the bathroom and the location of the hot-water tank?"

The old woman practically leapt from her chair for the opportunity to be helpful. He took in the surroundings with the speed of a lion studying his prey. The washroom would be ideal for the next step of the mission. He banged the hot-water tank and gave it some very official stares as he copied down the model number. He called out to Camilla from the end of the hall. "Is the water temperature hot? Turn it up please. We may have a problem." He marched down the hall with his flashlight in hand.

The old woman gave a pleading face. Who wouldn't do all they could for the possibility of free electricity? Glaaj gave the old woman a reassuring nod. The washroom was a standard five feet wide by ten deep. This made manoeuvring tight. As he shined his flashlight along the bottom of the bathtub, he asked her to step away from the sink and turn the tub water hotter. Camilla reached over Glaaj as he crouched and shone his flashlight along the bottom of the tub.

Camilla's scream was matched by the whoosh of air created by her falling body. Glaaj had wrapped his left arm around the old woman's ankles and placed his right forearm against her torso. He picked her up by taking her feet from under her and whipped her body straight back. The effect was the same as lifting a canoe paddle high in the air and slamming it against the water. There was a sickening crunch as her head connected with the edge of the tub. Camilla let out a soft moan as she drifted under water. With the length of a towel stretched out across her chest and arms like a rope, he held her body underwater until no more bubbles rose to the surface. Blood from the head wound turned the water a nice pastel pink that matched the rest of the home. The sound of water flowing into the tub brought satisfaction to Glaaj as he closed the door to the home.

Glaaj sat in his pick-up after the unpleasant task of removing the old woman's clothing. Which was in a trash bag that would later be burned up at the farm. He enjoyed his wild boar sandwich, overlooking the breathtaking Vera Cruz coastline. As he sipped his grape soda, a feeling of joy swelled inside him.

The evil inside him grew in size and appetite.

CHAPTER 45

GLAAJ'S PICKUP TRUCK was maintained on a shoestring budget. That afternoon the shoestring broke. The engine light turned on as steam billowed from under the hood. He pulled onto the shoulder along the Gulf Coast. As he raised the hood, he thought of worse places to breakdown, like the mosquito-infested bushes.

Water, water everywhere, but none for his truck. Saltwater would be murder on the engine. After the steam died off, it became apparent that the pressure release on the radiator cap had given way. The jug of water he kept behind the seat had only a couple cups left, not nearly enough for the truck. He opened up the garbage bag and removed the old woman's clothes. Draining the towel, shirt and pants gave him another couple of cups of water. It was still, not enough.

Glaaj draped the old woman's towel over the steering wheel and dash for protection from the sun. He locked the truck and, in the sweltering heat, started walking back to a remote village several kilometres back. Along the way he thought of how aggravated his father would be when he missed his afternoon chores.

The old communal hand pump ran freely and he filled his jug in five pumps. A few of the villagers gave friendly waves, but for the most part they were all enjoying their afternoon siestas. He drank several liters of water and filled his ball cap, drenching himself before heading back to the truck. The weight of the water made the trip back more of a test for the extremely fit male specimen. His breathing was only slightly faster than usual upon reaching the truck's door handle.

The towel had worked its magic, keeping the truck's interior relatively cool compared to the outside temperature. As he wiped his brow, he examined the rear truck-box and, to his horror, saw that the garbage bag was missing. His heart skipped a beat as he thought about the missing clothes, but only for a moment. He soon deduced that given the area and the poverty, some lucky woman just found a new outfit.

Under the cover of darkness, Glaaj approached Jeff's home back in Zempoala. After all the added mileage this week, the little pick-up seemed to sigh as it stopped. His afternoon chores were started late, and he was now late for his shift to watch Jeff. Maria greeted him with a kiss and a hug as he walked in the door. A feeling of pride swelled inside him as he stood beside Jeff's bed. His offering to aid Jeff's healing wasn't human blood this time. He pulled out the towel he had brought with him from a bag and lay the towel across Jeff's body in the same fashion as he did when killing the old woman.

Glaaj hoped the old woman's spirit would somehow transfer to Jeff through the towel. He whispered these words of encouragement, "May the spirits of your enemies make you well."

CHAPTER 46

EVEN DRESSED IN a three-piece suit, Jack Armstrong looked like a man whose level of depression exceeded any clinical diagnosis for hospitalization. He wore his hair long and scraggly, he'd stopped bathing weeks before and his organs were showing signs of chemical abuse. In short, his partnership with Cory Blake had been a life-altering experience. He looked at the interior of his sports car and felt ashamed that everything that had once mattered to him now seemed so pointless.

Reginald Cuthbert stepped out of his well-maintained Junction City family home and thought nothing of the dust-covered red sports car parked across the road. The elderly man had learned over time to place only half the amount of trash into his bags. It just made the job easier. A widower for the last ten years, he was thinking of assisted living. With winter on its way, time had a way of wearing him down.

"Mr. Cuthbert, how are you today sir?" Jack stepped out of his vehicle and approached the old man.

"Do I know you?" Cuthbert stopped and looked at him quizzically.

"Actually, I'm a friend of your neighbour's. They told

me you were interested in estate management. For just a moment of your time, I can show you how you could stay in your home forever. You can have professional care come right to your door. Best of all, there is no cost to you. Large pharmaceutical companies are lined up to pick up the majority of the cost."

Cuthbert's friends had been dying off at an alarming rate. Most of them were shipped off to hospitals to live out their last days in the sterility of a semi-private room. His family had all but forgotten him. At worst, he might have some company for a few minutes. "Sure, why don't you come in and tell me how it all works."

"Great, you won't regret this." Jack smiled. "Actually you are going to regret this a lot," he thought.

Reginald Cuthbert did not see the blow from the hammer as the two men entered the home. The depth of the wound at the back of his head ensured the man's death was instantaneous. Jack pulled a plastic bag out of his pocket and placed it over the head to contain the blood as he dragged the body to the bathroom. No sense in making a mess in his new home. After placing the body in the tub he went back to the car to retrieve his things.

From his bag he produced some of the finest German made surgical tools. After almost an hour's work, the body was dismembered and bagged. Just as he imagined, the old house had a freezer chest in the garage. He placed all of the parts into the freezer. Over the next several days he planned on delivering them to dumpsters throughout the Kansas City area.

The old Zenith television took a long time to warm up and the sound of the six o'clock evening news came on long before the picture. Jack made himself a sandwich while gulping a cold beer. He peered through the kitchen window curtains and observed his new next-door neighbour busily making his supper. Michael Thomson took no notice of his secret admirer.

CHAPTER 47

THE CALDERONE FAMILY stood in silence as the priest stood in front of a glossy brown casket covered in white flowers. The priest spoke to the small group of mourners. "And we are to be certain that Camilla Calderone is in a better place. For she sits at the right hand of our saviour Jesus Christ." A few of the women and children wept, although the majority felt she'd led a good life.

In the distance Glaaj observed the lovely ceremony. The news media made no mention of Mrs. Calderone's tragic death. Society just assumed it to be another elderly woman who slipped and died. Secretly, many in attendance were glad that she didn't survive to hang on in a coma until her body finally gave out. The ceremony ended as four men lowered the casket into the ground with ropes. Each member of the immediate family tossed dirt onto the casket below. They said their good-byes and headed for their vehicles.

This time, when Calderone approached his families' vehicle he took notice of the piece of paper under his windshield. The note said, "Minus three." He didn't understand the note, but he kept it in his pocket. His emotions were in a storm. He felt guilty leaving his mother behind during their family vacation. There just wasn't enough room in the caravan, what with the children getting bigger. She'd been so disappointed. He felt even worse when they got back and discovered her dead in the bathtub. The image of her bloated face haunts him to this day.

As the family went their separate ways after leaving the parking lot, Glaaj decided that the infliction of pain and suffering wasn't finished. He surmised Gonzola had been an accomplice. Calderone was the brain behind the operation, not to mention the driver on that fateful day. Glaaj observed whom Calderone spoke to most frequently during the ceremony. That was whom he was following now, a single man who drove a beat up pick-up truck much like his own.

The man pulled off the road up to a dilapidated shack in a remote area. Glaaj wondered why his friend didn't seem to be helping him out financially. When he saw the bottle of Tequila fall out of the truck and the man stumble out, it all made sense. He'd pickled himself over a twenty-minute drive. The man stumbled into his shack and collapsed onto the couch.

Glaaj removed the lift jack from the drunk man's rusted out truck and raised the front end. Using the lug wrench, he pulled off the front tire. A very unsteady drunk man finally came out to inquire about what was going on. "Hey what are you doing to my truck?"

Glaaj replied, "I was following you down the road when I noticed you had a newer tire than mine. Thought maybe if I took it you wouldn't mind."

Luckily, he was a mean drunk and came swinging at Glaaj. "Get away from my truck."

Glaaj took the opportunity and swung the lug wrench hard, connecting with his right temple. The drunken man fell like a ton of bricks. Glaaj swiveled his head around like a nervous owl, checking for witnesses. Seeing none, he dragged the man under the truck. Quickly, he lowered the truck onto the man's head and chest. There was a loud snapping sound as the vehicle's full weight collapsed the man's body. Glaaj re-raised the jack to the fully opened position and left it fallen over next to the vehicle for the police to find. As a final clue to the police, he hammered a nail into the side of the tire. He was certain the officer's comments would be, "Alcohol and mechanical work are a dangerous combination."

CHAPTER 48

HEAT SHIMMERED ON the horizon as Armand and Luis walked around the perimeter of the Martinez homestead. They looked at the beautiful home in the distance and admired their handiwork, but the look of concern on the older man's face spoke volumes. "Armand, I have noticed a change in you lately. Your father tells me you're working harder than ever. I am concerned that you have not dealt with the tragedy. Instead you seem to pretend like nothing has happened. You and Sophia were so close . . . "

"So you're concerned because I am continuing to live?" Armand cut him off.

Luis tried a new tactic. "Of course not. I just think that it is unhealthy to pretend like nothing has happened. People expect a certain amount of emotion when someone close to them dies. If you continue to act as if nothing happened, people will begin to talk."

"Let them talk. I deal with things in a way that allows me to sleep at night. Sophia died. Yes, I loved my cousin like a sister, but no amount of tears will bring her back. Now, let's go and see Jeff. I think your concern should be directed toward him." Armand blew him off.

Luis shook his head. He found this reasoning difficult to argue with. Together, the men walked up the front steps of the home. They reminisced as they looked over the home's construction. Luis held up his damaged hand and spoke of the difficulties he incurred from the beam construction accident. "I kick myself every time I look at my damaged hand. One stupid mistake can change you for the rest of your life. I guess it could've been much worse. I could've fallen and broken my neck and died." Luis looked around morosely. "This house was to be filled with the sounds of laughter and the squeals of screaming children. Instead there is only silence."

They said their hellos to Garcia, who stood in the kitchen and offered them coffee. They told him they'd come back for some after their visit with Jeff. They sauntered up the stairs and entered the master bedroom where the morning sun bored through the closed shutters. The two men opened them filling the room with brilliant sunshine. Immediately, they noticed Jeff's eyes were wide open and he had two black stripes on his cheeks that looked almost as if it was war paint. Luis waved his hand in front of Jeff's blank stare. "What the hell is going on? Is this grease on his face?" He walked over to the door and shouted down to Garcia. "Garcia come up here, please." Luis owed the catatonic man laying on the bed a debt of gratitude. To see him disrespected in this manner made his blood boil. When Garcia entered the room, Luis became aggressive. "Who did this? Is this some kind of joke?" Everyone was shocked to see the mild-mannered man so irate.

"I don't know what happened. An hour ago when I checked on him he was fine. Jesus was here earlier at sunup, talking with mom. Jeff sure as hell didn't have black grease on his face when I first came in this morning." Garcia tried to calm him down.

Luis fought the rage that quickly built inside him. No one would ever disrespect Jeff if he ever had anything to do with it. As far as he was concerned, Jeff saved his family from a long life of poverty and despair. The man should be treated as royalty. Not like some homeless man.

"All right, lets get him washed up. Jeff doesn't seem to be getting better. I'm worried for him." Luis took a deep breath.

CHAPTER 49

THE CALDERONE FAMILY stood in stunned silence as they listened to the news of their cousin Michael's death. It was somewhat ironic that the same incompetent officer who questioned Jeff about the death of Sophia and little Emily was delivering news to the Calderone's. Veronica rubbed her husband's back in a soothing motion as Anna and Jacob played outside in the morning dew.

The officer spoke in a serious tone while he adjusted his considerable girth. "Looks like after your cousin Michael left your mother's funeral, he drank himself silly. For whatever reason, he then decided to work on his pick-up. The truck was improperly jacked and the vehicle collapsed onto his body. When we looked in his home, we found your information listed as next of kin. I am sorry for your loss." The officer left the home.

Calderone turned and addressed Veronica. "Why is this happening? There seems to be this swirl of tragedy around me the last several weeks. My mother, now Michael."

"You are forgetting the Gonzolas." Veronica interjected.

"Yes, thank you dear. I hadn't forgotten about them.

They didn't die by accident though. And they weren't family. What I am trying to say is that there seems to be a cloud of disaster looming over my head. I didn't mention this to you before, but there was a note on my windshield when we left the funeral." He tried to hide his bitterness and passed his wife the note.

"Minus three. What do you make of it?" Veronica studied the note.

Calderone looked like a great thought had entered into his head. "What if this is someone's idea of a sick joke." He held up three fingers. "Three people who knew me are now dead."

"Or what if someone left the note on the wrong car? Honey, you're worrying me. You're sounding like someone who is going off the deep end. There can't be a link between this note and the deaths." Veronica looked at him skeptically.

"Maybe you're right." He gave her his wounded animal look. He walked across the room to put on his suit jacket. "I've got a meeting with Valadares in an hour. He has a lead for me on a parcel of land. He says the seller is very motivated. This means my first sale could be a big payday for us." He kissed his wife goodbye and thanked her for listening.

His blood ran cold as he slid behind the wheel of his car. There under the wiper blade, was a piece of paper. He removed it with trembling fingers and it read, "Minus four". He knew his wife's opinion on the matter and shoved the note in his breast pocket. He scanned the area for any potential onlookers. Seeing no one, he sped away.

From the cover of the bushes in an adjacent field, Glaaj watched. He wanted to jump with joy.

CHAPTER 50

CALDERONE PULLED UP to the real-estate head office outside of Vera Cruz with optimism on his side. He knew that the drive to the office every day would be a breeze. Everyone said that he would do well in the real-estate business. He looked forward to this day as he opened the door to the glass office building. Valadares pumped his hand. "Come to my office. I have your first assignment."

Calderone sat down in a nice leather chair. The only thing in the office that was unappealing was the smell of cigarette smoke that lingered in the air. Valadares spoke rapidly. "Calderone, I can't tell you how happy we are to have you on our team. With your knowledge of the area and the connections you have, you are going to be a real asset to our field office. I could see you doubling your salary within the first year."

Like everyone in the world Calderone enjoyed hearing about how he was going to do. He felt like everything was going to be more than okay. "Thank you for the vote of confidence, Señor. I won't let you down."

Valadares replied, "Great. Here is your first sale. There is a parcel of land that is an estate inheritance. I'm told the seller is looking to make a quick turnaround. That is very good for us. It's what we like to call a motivated seller. When you meet with him today, tell him you are willing to do the sale for a 25% commission. The land is two hours East of La Joya. Are you familiar with the area?"

"Yes. A hilly region. Not a lot of money. Not far from the coast. There is good opportunity for a resort. Does the land extend to the coast?" Calderone felt very excited.

"I like your thinking. The land does extend to the coast and as a famous Hollywood writer once wrote: If you build it, they will come. Feel free to use that in your pitch to potential buyers." Valadares smiled.

Calderone had completely forgotten about the note in his breast pocket. He thought about the potential for copious amounts of money. He'd send his children to the finest schools and get the largest diamond for his wife. "What time am I to meet the seller?"

Valadares pulled out his planner and handed a new planner to Calderone. "The directions and cell phone number are written down. You'll be meeting Peter Farrah this afternoon in the town center of La Joya. Don't be fooled by his rusted pick-up truck, not everyone flashes their money. I wouldn't choose to drive a fancy car if I didn't have this job. Worst investment any man can make."

Calderone stared out at his SUV and into his new leather-bound planner. "Peter Farrah, two o'clock. Again, I'm your man. I won't let you down."

CHAPTER 51

JACK ARMSTRONG FILLED his pages with sections of illegible words as he free handed with the spirit of Cory Blake. Every eighth or tenth page there would be a series of words that seemingly formed a sentence. Sleep had been foreign to him for months. There were dozens of spiral-bound notebooks stacked along the wall.

After months of work, Jack had pieced together the rest of Cory's instructions from the notes. The secrets of the afterlife would be unlocked once he finished the next series of tasks. Through the hole in the tin-foiled windows, he observed Michael getting into his small Japanese vehicle and driving off to work. He walked over to the freezer and examined the last pieces of Mr. Cuthbert's remains and reminded himself to take out the trash on his way to Kansas City.

Jack entered Michael's home with his equipment bag through the rear basement window. His high tech background made this next part of the operation as simple as breathing. Several hidden cameras were set up in the living area and bedroom. All the cameras were connected to a wireless router that would allow them to be remotely accessed from his computer in Mr. Cuthbert's dining room.

In the bedroom closet he found a few items vital to the completion of the mission. Several heirloom china place settings used by Natalie Brooks were set out on the dining table. Meals with their friends were eaten using these plates and Mrs. Brooks always said, "No sense letting nice dishes gather dust." The chips and missing flecks of colour were evidence of regular use. Jeff Brooks couldn't bring the set with him when he left; therefore he'd safely stored it before he'd boarded up the house.

Jack searched and found the extra set of keys to the home. On his way to dropping off Mr. Cuthbert's last remains he would also get copies of the house keys. Everything seemed to be in place for the evening's festivities. He secured all the windows and left using the back door. He was pleased with the brilliance of his plan. He had to take the first small steps to reunite the Junction City Four.

A bizarre chill went down his spine when he returned to the house. He turned on the computer, did a systems check and remotely controlled the cameras. He could feel that Cory was pleased with the completion of the first phase.

CHAPTER 52

GLAAJ WAITED IN the shade of a building in the town square of La Joya. So much preparation had gone into the meeting today that he felt like a little kid (receiving a birthday gift for the first time.) His excitement almost overwhelmed him when he spotted the black SUV pull into the town square. The few townspeople in the area looked impressed as they stared in the direction of the nice black vehicle.

He walked up to the SUV and tapped on the window. "You're late!" This statement was meant to throw off Calderone.

"Sorry. There was a road washout on my way. I had to double back and find a different route." Calderone hid his emotions well.

"You'd think with such a nice vehicle you could have driven through it. Oh well. I'm Peter Farrah, and if you haven't figured that out yet, you're not the man for this job. You'll have to follow me over to my land. If you can't keep up or follow, then turn around and go back to the city." Glaaj sneered.

"Sure thing, Señor Farrah." Calderone wasn't sure how

his new boss judged character, but the last description he would've used was 'nice'.

The drive into the remote area of La Joya proved to be a challenge for the four-wheel drive SUV. He drove in awe of the little old pickup truck. Oftentimes the vehicle balanced precariously on three wheels over rocks and logs. Even the most experienced four-wheel driver would consider the trail unmanageable. In the distance there was a waterfall and then a spectacular view of the coast. The pickup truck finally stopped.

The tall and muscular man stepped out of the pickup and waved in Calderone's direction. "This is what should sell this land. Paradise carved out of the jungle. I'll not negotiate with you on your commission. You'll get 30% and not a penny more."

Calderone now thought Peter Farrah really was nice. His new boss would be ecstatic when he heard of the commission. "Let me get the paperwork from my car. This access road will have to be cleaned out so potential buyers can come in more easily to see the view."

"Yes, I agree. I'll hire a team of men to get it done. There is another real selling point to this land. Follow me over to the waterfall." Glaaj nodded.

The hike to the waterfall proved to be an aggressive climb. The jungle dampness combined with the afternoon heat meant the two men were drenched in sweat. They reached a natural flat balcony next to the waterfall. The water spray made the rock slippery. The extra moisture created by the waterfall made the air hard to breathe. Glaaj called out. "Watch your step. It is dangerous up here." Next to the waterfall just above the ledge was a cave half the size of a prison cell. The walls were smoothly carved in the rock by water erosion over millions of years. Above the cave hung a large rock the size of a car. The rock looked like a hatch door waiting to be closed.

"Congratulations, Calderone. Let us say a toast to your future success in selling this land." Glaaj pulled two water bottles from his pack.

Calderone drank half the bottle in the first gulp. After a few seconds his balance betrayed him. "What's happening?" was all he managed to say as Glaaj grabbed him.

"Hold on there, Calderone. Wouldn't want you to slip and fall to your death too soon. I see the horse tranquilizer didn't agree with you. I think maybe you should rest awhile in this cave."

Glaaj pulled the man into the cave and quickly set the next stage of his plan into action. He hiked back down to the vehicles and retrieved two eight-foot lengths of four-inch ABS pipes. One of the pipes had a ninety-degree elbow with a large funnel cemented in place.

He brought the pipe back to the waterfall and proceeded to blast away the earth surrounding the large protruding rock hanging over the cave. The end of the pipe with the funnel was held under the powerful waterfall. To combat against the force of the water, Glaaj held the pipe with the assistance of ropes looped over his shoulders. Some believed this method of blasting away the earth beneath large rocks to move them was how Stonehenge's famous immovable rocks were erected. Like magic, the massive rock began to slowly fall into place, blocking the cave. The positioning of the rock was perfect. The gap between the rock and the cave opening was eight inches at the base and zero at the top, just like a leaning sheet of plywood.

Glaaj felt electricity in the air as he drove the black SUV deeper into the bush. He'd given the real-estate company bogus coordinates to the section of land. The chances of anyone stumbling into this area were very slim. He had to make it back for family chores before sundown. Calderone would be unconscious for at least another four hours.

CHAPTER 53

THE COOL FALL evening breeze hit Michael's open coat as he left the Tattoo You. Quickly, he grasped his coat's collar to close it. At that moment he thought of Jeff. His friend had missed their last scheduled phone call. Not too unusual, given the difficulties in communication from Zempoala, not to mention how busy he must be with a toddler and a wife. Still, he wondered how Jeff was doing in the beautiful warmth of his Mexican paradise. He could guarantee that he wasn't clutching at his coat to try and stay warm.

He drove back to where he was living at Jeff's home. There was something about living there that made Michael very happy. It was not just the big screen television, satellite and awesome sound system. It was all those memories of wild parties and good friends that remained in the home. "Home is where the heart is." He thought. Michael certainly agreed with whoever had said that. Living with his parents all those years had stifled who he really was. This was one of the best things that had ever happened to him.

He entered the darkened home and turned on the light in the living room. Everything looked much as it had when he left. As he went to grab a beer from the kitchen, he stopped dead in his tracks. The setting on the table looked like it was pulled right out of his memory. The only thing missing was Mrs. Brooks coming around the corner to greet him with a warm hug. Michael felt a chill.

He went from room to room checking locks and windows. Everything looked untouched. Everything, that was except for the dining room table that he stared at from a distance. Part of him felt that if he were to touch the dishes they would disappear like a mirage. Hunger overcame his puzzlement and he devoured leftovers as he stood in the kitchen staring at the dining room table.

Although still filled with uncertainty, Michael went and sat down in the living room to watch the evening news. After the news was finished, he decided he was being silly and removed the dishes from the table and stacked them on the counter. He scratched his head, still trying to figure out how this could have happened. Giving up on solving the mystery, he turned off the lights in the kitchen and settled into some of his favourite shows on television.

Jack sat in front of his computer, observing everything from Michael's house. The little cameras worked their magic. The look of shock on Michael's face was priceless. Jack flicked a switch and a hidden solenoid he had placed at the back of a cupboard pushed the bottom of the rear panel forward. Michael's dishes spilled out of the cupboard and smashed onto the floor. Jack laughed as he watched Michael dance around the room in panic, searching for the ghost of Mrs. Brooks.

CHAPTER 54

GLAAJ RETURNED TO his imprisoned enemy with an extra bounce in his step. This time the climb up to the waterfall's ledge proved effortless. He was just unfolding a hunting chair next to the large rock blocking the cave opening when he heard the screams of his prisoner. The roar of the waterfall meant that no one else would hear his screams. He sat against the wall next to the eight-inch opening.

"Hola, Calderone." Glaaj spoke into the opening as if he were greeting a long lost friend.

A forehead and a pair of eyes appeared in the gap. There was tremendous relief in Calderone's voice. "Oh my God. Thank you. Peter Farrah is that you? Thank God you are here. What happened? Was there an avalanche? I can't remember a thing. I thought I was going to die here for sure. Please help me get out of here."

"Yes, I've come with good news. The authorities are on their way to save you." Glaaj smirked at the man's optimism.

Calderone was relieved. "That's fantastic. When will they be here? How long have I been here? What happened?"

"So many questions. Well, here's the thing. You seemed very exhausted from the climb up to the waterfall. You grew tired and went for a nap in the cave. That's when this boulder fell, blocking the opening." Glaaj found this all very amusing.

"I never went for a nap. What's going on here?" Calderone sounded skeptical.

"You're right. You caught me in a lie. I drugged you, put you in the cave and entombed you for safekeeping." Glaaj laughed like a madman.

"No! Why have you done this? Let me out of here!" Calderone started screaming frantically, trying to reach Glaaj with one arm protruding from the opening.

Glaaj grabbed the arm with a vice-like grip and pulled out a knife. He sliced the man's meaty palm and held it there as blood poured into a cup. Calderone pulled on his arm and screamed in agony. When Glaaj let go of the arm it slithered back into the cave like a dew worm retreating from an unfamiliar touch.

"Calderone give me your hand back or we are going to have problems." Glaaj screamed into the opening. No hand appeared. "Maybe I should come back with the blood of your seven-year-old son, Jacob, or your nine-year-old daughter, Anna?" The arm tentatively reappeared. "That's better." He wrapped the wound with a pressure bandage and taped the arm gently. He spoke softly with sorrow in his voice. "You can take your arm back now."

"You leave my family out of this, whatever the hell *this* is." Calderone screamed in confusion. "Why are you doing this?"

Glaaj laughed once more at his feisty prisoner. "You

really don't know? You killed Sophia Brooks Martinez and her little princess Emily when you and your blood-sucking friend visited Zempoala for more money. When you were turned away by Jeff, who by the way is one of the greatest men I've ever known, your careless driving on the muddy roads took two innocent lives. You even have a small dent in the rear of your vehicle to prove your guilt. You never even stopped."

Calderone felt something crawl across the back of his neck. He swiped it away in a panic with his hands hitting the cave wall. Pain shot up through his arm as his damaged hand throbbed.

"I swear, I didn't know. You have to believe me. Please let me go. I beg you. I thought the dent happened in a parking lot." Calderone cried in anguish.

"Why would I let you go? The fun is just beginning. Besides, aren't you in the least bit curious who will be minus five?" Glaaj laughed sadistically.

He packed up and left as the roar of the waterfall washed out the screams in the distance.

CHAPTER 55

GLAAJ MARCHED UP the steps to Jeff's home for his overnight shift. Al and Luis sat at the kitchen table playing cards. Al spoke to Glaaj, "Good, you're here. We've been a little concerned with your lateness these past few days."

"Sorry. I've been very busy with someone new in my life." Glaaj apologized simply.

"Tell us all about her." Luis and Al were very pleased.

"Another time. For now I would like to pay my respects to Jeff." Glaaj smiled.

The old men nodded simultaneously, understanding without speaking. Al added these encouraging words. "Dr. Wolfe left around an hour ago. He administered a drug called Benzodiazepine. He hopes that Jeff will begin his road to recovery today. The warning he gave us was that it is still up to Jeff though."

This sliver of hope brought joy to Glaaj's heart. "I'll stay very close to him. Promise." With that, he proceeded up the stairs as the two men packed up and left for home.

Glaaj pulled out his container and began his ritual of

willing Jeff back to health with the spirits of his enemies. In the darkened room he chanted in a monotone voice. "May the blood of your enemies make you healthy and whole again." As he repeated these words, he placed drops of Calderone's blood on his forehead, shoulders and wrists. "May the blood of your enemies make you healthy and whole again. May the blood of your enemies make you . . . " Just as he finished applying blood to his chest, two hands flew up with lighting speed and gripped Glaaj's arms. He let out an involuntary yelp.

For the first time in over a month, Jeff Brooks spoke. "What are you doing? What's going on?" Glaaj noticed the look of fear and confusion on his face.

Glaaj quickly recounted the horrid tale, ending with, "And then you had a bonfire on the beach, lighting yourself on fire. Jesus tackled you into the water and saved your life. You were carried into the house and Dr. Wolfe says you've been catatonic ever since." He waited and let the silence hang. "Let me get you a wet towel to wipe up your sweat." He didn't want to alarm Jeff with the blood all over his body.

In the dim light he was unaware of the tears streaming down Jeff's face. He gently wiped away the blood from Jeff's body. The warm towel easily soaked it all up. Again Jeff's hand grabbed his forearm. With a croak in his throat he spoke. "Why are you doing this?"

Glaaj looked at him with remorse. "You changed all our lives. You're part of the family. If you'd never come here, we would all have been poor forever. You've helped more people than you realize. You overpaid workers out of the kindness of your heart. That money went not only to those men, it trickled down into their families as well.

Everyone is terribly saddened by what has happened to you and your family. Maria has stayed by your side praying for you. She will be overjoyed with your recovery. We all will be."

Jeff asked him to help him sit up, get out of bed and go to the washroom. As he helped him into the washroom, Jeff spoke. "What have I become? Everyone I've loved goes away in the end." He then produced long, heaving, deep sobs, the kind of anguish that cannot be described with words, but felt, like the edge of a knife.

Glaaj supported his friend in his pain. A tear slowly rolled down his cheek and dropped onto Jeff's shoulder. A singular thought began to scream inside him. Calderone would pay for his crimes. In the end, he would pray for death.

Glaaj's evil spirits had a hunger that must be fed. He could feel it throb like a pounding headache.

CHAPTER 56

ICHAEL FINISHED INKING a very pretty girl named Amy, who wanted a rose and heart covered in thorns on her hip. "These are the perks of the job," he told himself. The tattoo was her way of rebelling against her overbearing parents. The reason for tattoos always interested him greatly. Most were in remembrance of a family member or loved one that had passed away. He felt honoured to help record history in such a unique way.

He'd learned the gift of gab from his mother and it seemed the prettier the client the more he spoke. This was probably due to his nervousness around the opposite sex. He'd also inherited his mother's physique, constantly battling his weight. Maybe a job where he sat around all day wasn't the best idea for his health, but as he stared at Amy's perfect pelvis, he decided it was worth the sacrifice.

"So, do you live alone Mike?" Amy asked, with a voice that could melt butter.

"Normally I would answer yes to that. Tell me, do you believe in ghosts?" Michael sighed.

"My grandparent's home was haunted out in the

155

country. We'd all be sitting in the family room when we'd hear footsteps in the upstairs bedroom. Nobody else was upstairs though. Very spooky stuff. Why do you ask?"

Michael looked into her soft blue eyes. He had to tell someone about what was going on. "I live in my friend's house. Kinda like house-sitting while he's out of the country. The other night, when I came home, his mother's china was set out on the kitchen table, just the way his mother used to for special dinners with friends, right down to the number of place settings. But, you see, his mother died a while ago. I'm not going to lie to you, I'm a little freaked out."

"That's creepy. I feel so bad for you. Has anything else weird happened?" Amy stared at him in shock, but her curiosity pushed her to ask the question.

"Actually, all of my dishes were pushed out of the cupboard and smashed on the floor that same night. I've also been hearing weird noises throughout the house. Sounds that are like a woman's footsteps with high heels. I feel like I'm losing my mind." Michael took a deep breath.

Amy gave out a soft whimper. "You should really talk to a psychic or someone who specializes in the paranormal. If I knew anyone like that I'd help you out, but I don't. Sorry." Michael covered up her tattoo with cellophane and told her to apply ointment morning and night. She left the tattoo parlor and Michael locked up and drove home.

As he walked into the house, he noticed muddy high-heeled footprints leading down the hall. When he walked by the dining room, he saw the china set out on the table.

CHAPTER 57

TWO DAYS HAD passed since Glaaj had last visited his prisoner. The musty smell of rotting vegetation wafted into his nostrils as he approached the waterfall. The scenery surrounding him promoted serenity and peace. Yet, only hatred and anger lay deep down in his heart.

Calderone felt something crawling on his shoulder and his survival instincts made him reach around to grab it. He grew excited as the large spider squirmed in his grasp. He squashed the spider's head with a rock and brought the spider up to his mouth. He needed food. He was beyond hungry. Just then he heard something outside the cave.

Glaaj unfolded his chair and sat next to the opening, he heard hoarse whispers from Calderone. "Please, you must help me. I need water. You can't let me die like this." The stench from the cave came from the fecal matter that had been pushed through the opening.

"Whoever said I was going to let you die? Calderone, it must be very difficult for you to sit and listen to millions of gallons of fresh water rushing by your cave and know that you can't taste a drop of it. Must be maddening!"

Glaaj laughed and handed him a small bottle of water that was only an eighth full. "You should try to make that water last." Next he passed him a container with raw meat that had been pureed. "The protein in the meat should help you."

"Please, fill the water bottle from the waterfall? I beg you." The bottle of water reappeared in the opening, empty.

Glaaj grabbed the water bottle from his hand and filled it up letting the water splash all over his body. "So you would like me to leave you this full bottle of water?"

"Yes!" Calderone hoarsely screamed his reply.

He pulled out a pair of pliers from his back pocket. "Well, I am nothing if not a fair man. Here is the deal I am willing to make you. If you would like this bottle of water, you will have to take these pliers and pull out a tooth of your choice."

"You're mad. I'll do no such thing." Calderone's eyes went wide as he stared at the man from the base of the eight-inch opening.

"I can almost guarantee that you will." Glaaj gave him words of encouragement.

"Never!" Calderone answered defiantly.

Glaaj gave him more words of encouragement as he looked over his notes from when he broke into Calderone's house. "Yesterday, when I followed Jacob and Anna to St. Joseph private school they seemed sad. Almost like they were missing someone in their lives. Maybe if I were to bring you their teeth it would make you listen?"

The look of total terror in Calderone's eyes brought joy to his heart. He waved the pliers in front of the man's terrified eyes. Calderone's eyes disappeared from view and an arm jutted out. "Give me the pliers." He said hoarsely.

Glaaj listened intently to the screams of pain coming from the cave as the man ripped out a tooth with the pliers. After the screams had ended, Glaaj yelled into the cave. "Give me the tooth and the pliers now!" Calderone did as he was told. His eyes then came into view again. Calderone spoke in a weakened tone. "Water. Please, give me the water."

Glaaj laughed as he spoke, inches away from the man's face. "Good. I think you are starting to understand how our relationship is going to work. As promised, I will leave you the water bottle." Glaaj stepped back and placed the water bottle in the man's sight line, four feet out of his reach. "Now you will have the bottle of water to entertain you as well as the sound of torrents of fresh water. You should really learn to negotiate better in the future. I've left you the water bottle as promised. Do not question me next time when I ask you to do something." Glaaj left with an extra bounce in his step. The sounds of tormented screams were in concert with the powerful waterfall.

CHAPTER 58

D R. WOLFE PLACED the blood pressure unit back in his bag. He stared into Jeff's eyes, waving the penlight back and forth. As he spoke to Jeff, he kept a positive tone in his voice. "Jeff, you are a very lucky man with many reasons to live. These people you've helped love and respect you. I can't begin to imagine what you've been through emotionally, but you have to draw on the people around you that clearly love you."

"Right now, all I want to do is swim out into the Gulf and never come back." Jeff sat up in his bed and held his head in his hands. Tears rolled down his cheeks freely.

Dr. Wolfe looked at him with concern. "So, you are still suicidal then?" Jeff simply nodded. "Would you be willing to take some medication for the next little while?" Jeff sobbed and nodded. The man had reached his breaking point. Dr. Wolfe knew there was no chance of Jeff recovering if he went to a hospital. In fact, he believed remaining here surrounded by people who wanted to care for him was a much better option. He handed Jeff two pills and a glass of water. "I am going to leave some antidepressants for you to take morning and night. You are going to have to eat, do some walking and talk about how you are feeling. Remember Jeff, time heals all wounds, inside and out." He lightly tapped Jeff on the shoulder and left the room.

Dr. Wolfe spoke to the crowd of people in the living room. Everyone waited to hear the good news of Jeff's recovery, including Glaaj. "Jeff is in a very delicate state. He will need your love and support if he is to recover. I've left instructions on the refrigerator for his medication. Please remember to always reassure him and let him know how you are feeling as well. He will only recover with your love and support." Since Dr. Wolfe didn't announce a clean bill of health, he left without much fanfare.

The group who now considered themselves immediate family went upstairs to see Jeff. Garcia, Luis, Al, Armand, Jesus and Maria entered the room. Maria sat on the bed and held Jeff in a long embrace. One of the men, Glaaj, went over and fluffed Jeff's pillow. In doing so, he palmed Calderone's tooth and shoved it inside the pillowcase. Under his breath he murmured, "May the pains of your enemies make you healthy and whole." He smiled at Jeff and patted him on the shoulder.

The group managed to make Jeff smile as they reminisced about their beautiful Sophia. Together they assisted him in a walk along the beach. Afterwards, they enjoyed a nice light breakfast overlooking the Gulf Coast. The sounds of the ocean, the heat of the sun, along with the first effects of the medication, made Jeff feel normal again. Still, as he stared out into the Gulf, all he wanted was to swim to the ocean floor.

CHAPTER 59

MICHAEL THANKED GOD that his last tattoo of the day was a simple memorial plaque. The soldier wanted to remember his final tour of duty. He'd been rattled over the last several days by the events inside the house. The weird noises and furniture rearrangements were seriously affecting his psyche. He finally heard a voice through his distractions, "Are you always this focused when doing a tattoo?"

Michael apologized, "Sorry, I've had a lot on my mind these last several days. There's weird paranormal stuff happening at the home where I'm staying. It's gotten so bad that I'm thinking of moving back into my parents' place until I can find somewhere else to live. The problem is, I can't abandon my duty to my friend."

"Well, that's not an excuse you hear every day. A problem with the old lady, yes, not problems with a haunted house." The soldier chuckled to himself.

"Sorry I brought it up." Michael felt immediately embarrassed, wishing he could have jammed the words back into his mouth. He placed cellophane over the tattoo, went through the usual maintenance spiel and thanked the soldier for his business. As the soldier stepped out into the evening air, the muscular figure of Jack Armstrong strolled into the parlour. Michael felt a chill run straight up his spine. "Get out!" was all he managed to say.

"Listen, before you call the cops, I came to say I'm sorry. I never should have tormented you the way I did. Just give me a moment of your time to explain and we can sort everything out. I promise. Let me buy you a beer. I just want you to hear me out." Jack held up his arms in a surrendering posture.

Michael mulled it over for a few minutes. Quite frankly, the thought of going back to the Brooks house and rediscovering the china set out again wasn't very appealing. With caution in his voice Michael said, "Meet me at the back of Club Yesterday by the pool table in half an hour."

Jack seemed genuinely excited, "You won't regret this, I promise. What I have to tell you is going to make you understand everything." He left and headed for his car.

Half an hour later Michael walked into Club Yesterday to a hail of 'Hey Michael' from several people he'd not seen in years. To his surprise the place hadn't changed much. The old license plates still hung from the rafters, along with the canoe paddles and twinkling lights. He found Jack with a pitcher of beer and two mugs waiting patiently by the pool table.

"I'm sorry. I'm truly sorry." Jack pumped his hand with a handshake.

"What brought on this new revelation?" Michael smiled at the sudden change.

Jack listened to Cory's voice in his head, which told him exactly how to act and what to say. "When I first dabbled in the dark arts and stumbled onto Cory Blake, I had no idea what I'd gotten myself into. I mean, look at me now compared to what I was a few weeks ago. Last time you saw me, I was on the verge of a nervous breakdown. Nobody wants that kind of a life."

"Yeah you really freaked me out." Michael nodded.

Jack continued, "Right. You see though, I managed to start my own sort of side business. I've got to tell you it's way more exciting than computers. Ever since you gave me this wonderful tattoo on my back, it's enabled me to walk into a room and feel the presence of spirits. Not only that Michael, I can speak to them. I've learned to use my talents for good. I can communicate with the spirits and find out what is keeping them here. I was able to sort things out for Cory and let his spirit leave this earth. I basically sort out their problems and allow them to continue on their journey."

"I accept your apology. Tell me, do you believe in fate?" Michael felt as if a million watt light bulb had gone on in his head.

Jack smiled, knowing full well that his cock and bull story had just been swallowed hook, line and sinker. Now he only had to reel the big fish in. "Fate and many other things, Michael."

CHAPTER 60

GLAAJ APPROACHED THE waterfall with renewed hope for his friend Jeff. Deep down he believed that his offerings to Jeff had not only brought him out of his catatonic state, but also made him healthier. The walk along the beach had renewed his belief that he was doing the right thing. Calderone's suffering was making Jeff stronger.

Steam rose from the ground as the afternoon heat dried the night's rain. He peered into the opening of the cave and saw Calderone's face. A day and a half had elapsed since his last visit. His prisoner's eyes were closed and his skin colour looked ashen. He grabbed a stick and poked the man in the forehead. His eyes flew open. Glaaj spoke with friendliness in his voice. "Good, you're not dead. You had me worried. When I was a small boy hunting in the woods my uncles taught me the rule of three. The rule is very simple; an average man cannot survive three minutes without air, three days without water or three weeks without food. You had me worried when I saw your grey skin. I thought maybe you were going to be the exception to the rule. After all, what fun would I have if you were delirious and unaware of my presence. Today I will give you energy and life so that you'll fully understand the pain you caused Jeff Brooks."

Calderone could only whisper, "Water." His physical strength had deteriorated at an alarming rate. For days now he'd been suffering from headaches and cramps. As professional athletes suffer from cramps in their muscles from lack of hydration, so did Calderone. His internal organs battled for survival.

When a full bottle of water and a container of food came through the opening, Calderone drank greedily. He coughed and sputtered the water. Glaaj spoke to him through the opening. "Drink slowly or your stomach will reject the water. It's strange, how stupid the body can be. I've brought you extra protein. I even added spices to the meat to make it more edible."

The water lubricated his throat and turned his whisper into an audible voice. "Why the sudden change of heart? I thought you were enjoying watching me die?"

"Your usefulness hasn't ended. How is the meat? Remember, eat it slowly or your body will reject it." Glaaj laughed.

He waited approximately an hour for Calderone to finish his water and meat. "Pass the containers back to me please." As the containers were handed back, Glaaj asked about the man's wife. "Your wife, her name is Veronica Calderone, correct?" Calderone simply nodded. "She is a very pretty woman as I recall, or should I say, was. I'm very saddened to inform you that she was minus five. The fifth casualty in the war you started. "

"No, no, no! You are lying. Tell me you are lying." Calderone's eyes welled up with tears as he stared through the rock opening.

Glaaj spoke in a condescending tone, "If you cry, you are wasting your body's precious fluids." He held up the lid of the container for him to see. Calderone's eyes widened as he noticed the large "Minus five" written on the lid. He had not seen it due to the dim light in the cave and his overpowering hunger. Glaaj added the deathblow, "By the way, how did she taste?"

The screams of insanity mixed with the sounds of vomiting brought glee to Glaaj's heart. He yelled into the opening. "The body is so stupid, wasting all those precious fluids and protein it needs to survive."

As he hiked back down to his truck, Glaaj thought Jeff would certainly be back to his old self after the torment that Calderone had just been put through.

CHAPTER 61

Jack Armstrong rang the doorbell and waited on the stoop. The door to the bungalow opened slowly. Michael stood half asleep in the living room. He scratched himself and looked out into the morning sun, "Kind of early isn't it?" He waved to the china set still out on the dining room table.

Jack gave a friendly chuckle and began speaking excitedly. "Ah, the dishes you told me about. Contrary to people's beliefs, most spirits are receptive in the early morning hours. Just last week I dealt with a young couple whose home was haunted by an old Indian spirit by the name of Chaske. Turns out this poor fellow was taken out back and repeatedly whipped until he died from the infections in the cuts on his back. All his focus and anger was aimed towards the bullring attached to the wall of the home. That bullring is where they tied the poor young man's hands. You know what a bullring is? You see them in barns. A metal ring attached to the wall to pass a rope through. The husband and wife would hear this ring clang at times but had no clue as to why. Once I explained it to them, they said it all made sense. Chaske also had ice-cold water dumped on him in the dead of winter as he hung from the bullring. When I told the couple this news they went pale and gasped. They told me that people who entered the home and passed by the ring would complain of a sudden feeling of ice water being dumped on them."

Jack continued setting the stage, padding his resume. "Now, Chaske was never going to leave that land. Simply put, he'd experienced such horror that the young man could never have another rational thought. He'd become a deranged animal, much like an attack dog that will attack on command because of all the abuse he's suffered. Do you know what the solution was?"

"I have no idea what the solution was. I couldn't even begin to guess." Michael answered.

Jack laughed in triumph, "It was the bullring. All his focused anger involved that bullring. I knew we couldn't simply throw the bullring away or else Chaske would fixate on something else. So I had the husband screw the bullring on a tree in the rear of the yard. That did it. No more disruptions in the house. That's when I knew that your tattoo on my back gave me special spiritual powers. Michael, that tattoo is a gift. Thank you."

At that moment two police cars pulled into the neighbour's driveway, the very same neighbour that Jack Armstrong had killed and dismembered. Thankfully, all the tools used in the crime had been bleached that same day, rinsed the next day, chlorinated the following day and then rinsed again. The only evidence that existed in the home that might lead the officers to the killer was the computer with links to the cameras observing Michael's home. Jack had learned to take it all in stride.

"Michael, I'll need space to wander around through

the rooms and get the spirit to contact me. I've discovered that the spirits follow similar patterns in death as they did in life. Therefore the morning is the best time to deal with them. I know it sounds strange, but I'll need you to step outside. You see, removing yourself from the house will enable the spirit to focus on me and not you." Jack smiled.

Michael quickly got dressed and stepped out into the cool Junction City morning air as instructed by Jack. Constable David Hill of the Junction City Police Force took notice of him and waved. He strode over and asked Michael about his neighbour. "When was the last time you saw Mr. Cuthbert?"

"You know, now that you mention it, at least a week or so. He's not dead is he?" Michael scratched his right ear as he thought.

"Why do you think he's dead?" Constable Hill tilted his head and looked expectantly at him.

"I just meant that he was an older man. I haven't seen him in a while. Good, so he's not dead." Michael backtracked quickly.

Hill could see that Michael wasn't a suspect, and had no useful information. "It's an ongoing investigation. His second cousin in Milwaukee has been trying to reach him and thought it strange that he hadn't called her back. That's when she called us. If you see him around or see someone around the house, give us a call." Hill handed him a business card.

"Will do officer." Michael nodded.

Meanwhile, back in the home, Jack had finished removing all of the cameras from the home. Later, from his car, he'd remotely wipe the computer hard-drive clean with his laptop. He waited patiently for Michael to come back into the house.

The door opened and Michael stepped in with a look of shock on his face. "My neighbour Mr. Cuthbert has gone missing. The cops just asked me when I saw him last. This is very strange."

Jack gave him a friendly tap on the shoulder. "Well, I have very good news for you. I made contact with the spirit. You won't believe this. She is the woman who lived in this house and her name is Natalie."

"It's true then, a woman named Natalie used to live here when I was younger." Michael sat down hard on the couch. "How did you do it?"

"I told you, it's the tattoo that you put on my back. It's like a portal for the spirit world." Jack smiled.

"What did she say?" Michael stared at him in disbelief.

Jack knew that Cory was somewhere, at that very minute, dancing with joy. He didn't know where, though. He had as much connection with the spirit world as a desk lamp. Cory had selected him, tormented him into doing his bidding and never let go. What kept Jack going was the belief that all the secrets to the afterlife were going to be his as soon as the last phase of his mission ended. Cory had promised him.

Jack continued, "She said a lot of things. At first she was hard to understand. Natalie died in a car accident and never had a chance to say good-bye to her son Jeff. She's mad that he hasn't been here. The dishes have been set out in hopes of his return. Every day that he doesn't arrive, she gets more and more upset." He sighed to emphasize the sadness.

A questioning look crossed Michael's face. "But, Jeff lived here for months after his mother died. Why didn't she just say good-bye to him then? Why get mad at me? It's not my fault that Jeff left. Really, I'm here as a favour to him, just house-sitting until he gets back." Jeff's whereabouts were still a secret to everyone except Michael.

Jack's smile faded a little. "When Jeff lived here she didn't want to leave. In her mind, when he was here, she kept on living her life. She watched her son live his life. There was no reason for her to leave. When Jeff left and boarded her up inside the house, she became trapped and angry. Simply put, she was like a caged animal. When you moved in, it was like a coiled spring being released. While you remain here without Jeff," he paused for effect. "you may be in danger."

"What should I do?" Michael turned as white as a ghost.

Jack didn't need to be clairvoyant to see that his plan had worked. "Let me try and speak to her." He stared up to the light fixture and spoke. "You must give Michael peace. Leave him until he can bring Jeff back." He looked at Michael and asked, "How long will it take you to bring Jeff back?"

"Maybe in a month or two. It's really difficult to get in touch with him. I'll try my hardest." Michael gave him a confused look.

Jack stood a little straighter. "Natalie, give us a sign if this is acceptable." He pulled on the fishing line he'd tucked behind the sofa, attached to a deck of playing cards. The cards tumbled from the top shelf of the wall unit. The queen of hearts landed face up and Jack quickly collected the cards from the ground and retrieved his fishing line. He turned to Michael and added, "This is good. Natalie agrees to leave you alone. Call me when Jeff arrives so I can mediate. Also, she says to leave the china set out."

Jack left the house confident that all the pieces of the plan were falling into place nicely.

CHAPTER 62

CALDERONE SPENT MOST evenings huddled in madness with insects biting and crawling on his skin. The cave was too short for him to lie in and too low to stand. This meant that his body constantly stiffened and he felt like one giant bruise. He reached out and touched various points in the cave in a repetitive pattern in an attempt to stretch out his sore limbs. Pain had become his only companion.

He tried to remember his children's faces and the sounds of their voices to combat his growing madness. He thought of his dead wife, how her hair smelled of fruit and her skin felt velvety soft. She did not deserve the horrible death she must have experienced, only to be dismembered and served as food for her husband. He pushed out the negative thoughts that made him wonder if his children were safe from the mad man who had placed him in this cave.

A hissing coming from the opening of the cave interrupted his thoughts. In the dim light of the evening he observed the snake approach. Slowly and cautiously it moved toward him in search of warmth. He felt for a rock along the edge of the cave. The snake inched closer.

None of the rocks were large enough to do any damage. With his good hand he ignored his pain and quickly grabbed the snake behind the head. The snake contorted and hissed as it tried to bite his arm. The strength of it surprised him as he began repeatedly mashing the head into the cave wall until it stopped moving.

He bit into the tough skin and pulled to expose the meat of the snake. As he ate the flesh, he fought his body's instinct to vomit. When he could not stand another bite he coiled the rest of the snake in the corner of the cave and thought about how long the meat would last un-refrigerated.

The sounds of laughter filled the cave as the thought of having food to spoil made him realize the insanity of his situation. His laughter turned to crying as he realized the insanity of his situation; then the sound of screaming filled the cave.

CHAPTER 63

JEFF WATCHED THE dust particles suspended in the air do a slow dance in the morning sunlight. Ever since he had been a small boy, he had never understood how the dancing particles in the brilliant sunshine seemed to be never-ending. The antidepressants were taking effect nicely. Jeff no longer wanted to take an endless swim into the Gulf. That's not to say that he wasn't terribly saddened by the state of his life, but at least now he could walk along the beach every morning without the thought of suicide. He listened to what Dr. Wolfe had said and watched what he ate and drank. The scars left on his body were badges of his grief.

He rolled over on his pillow, reached under it with his right hand, and felt something hard. He lifted the pillow and looked underneath. There was nothing there. He was certain he'd felt something. Then he spotted the bump inside his pillowcase. He reached in and pulled it out. "What the hell is this doing in my pillow?" He said as he held a human tooth with the root still attached between his thumb and forefinger. The dust particles danced in the background. He placed the tooth on the bedside table and went downstairs.

Garcia lay asleep on the sofa. He stirred as Jeff walked by. "Good morning," he mumbled. Jeff stopped and looked at him. "Garcia, why do you insist on sleeping on the couch? There are other beds for you to use in this house."

"This couch is the most comfortable thing I've ever slept on." Garcia stood and stretched.

Jeff shrugged. "Suit yourself. Come grab some coffee, I found something weird upstairs and I need your opinion."

On the table there was a pile of mail. He spotted a letter from Michael and he tore it open. His body language must have shown his agitation as he read the urgent request for his return to Junction City.

"Is everything okay Jeff?" Garcia asked.

Jeff nodded. He couldn't believe what he had just read. He'd have to take a ride into Zempoala later that day and speak with Michael on the phone.

Jeff remembered what he'd found in his pillow and spoke to Garcia. "I found a human tooth in my pillow case this morning. Now, I stopped believing in the tooth fairy a long time ago. No one is going to convince me there is some kind of a reverse tooth fairy giving back teeth." He sighed. "Do you have any idea how it got there?"

"You found the tooth in your pillow? That is very strange." Garcia shook his head.

Jeff saw that Garcia didn't seem to have any information about the tooth, so he carried on to more pressing matters. "Are you busy today? I'd like to go into town and make a phone call to Michael."

Garcia agreed. "That is a great idea. We'll take my

truck. If you are up to it, I will take you on a ride up the coast afterward. There is an area that I have been baiting for a month. There is lots of activity. I think the boar is more than one hundred kilograms."

"Sure, I think all that fresh air would do me some good. I'll pack some food and drinks." Jeff replied.

CHAPTER 64

JEFF HANDED THE man behind the counter in the corner store some American cash for his phone call to Michael. The conversation left him numb. His thoughts of home were coming to him in a massive flood. Could his mother really be communicating with his close friend? Was his mother truly tormented by his departure? He felt so guilty. He wanted to rush home immediately and do what he could for his mother's ghost. It all sounded so bizarre.

Garcia's voice broke his train of thought. "How is my drinking buddy, Michael, doing? You look troubled my friend. What is it?"

Jeff thought of the far-fetched tale he'd just heard over the phone. How could he express what he'd just heard without sounding crazy? "Garcia, have you ever heard people talk of spirits and ghosts?"

Garcia nodded with enthusiasm, "My mother told me the story of her brother's death. After his passing she went to his house by herself, sat on the bed and cried. She felt a hand on her shoulder that startled her. When she looked up, she saw her brother with a smile on his face. She told me that the expression on his face made her tears of sadness turn to tears of joy. She knew that he was in a better place."

Jeff suddenly felt much better about sharing his strange tale. "Michael just told me that he is being bothered by my mother's spirit. Apparently she is tormented by my departure to Mexico. She needs to say good-bye to me before she can continue on her journey to the afterlife." Jeff shook his head.

"That's heavy stuff. How are you handling it?" Garcia looked at him in disbelief.

"It seems that every time I take one step forward I fall ten steps back. It's one bloody thing after another. I have to deal with this. I have no choice. I must go see Michael." Jeff sighed.

Garcia carefully chose his next words, "Before you do that, let me take you to a special place where the scenery is so breathtaking that it will clear your mind and your lungs. You'll know exactly what to do after this trip. What do you say?"

Jeff had forgotten about the planned trip. His mind was such a jumble. He wouldn't be able to make travel arrangements today if he went. Every fibre in his being wanted to say no. But, when he looked into Garcia's puppy dog eyes, his position changed. "Why not. Looks like I can use all the help I can get."

They piled back into the truck and headed toward the mountains, following the switchback roads the higher they climbed. The term switchback comes from the constant zigzag pattern created by the road as it climbs the mountainside. The higher they drove, the more breathtaking the scenery became.

"So, where are we heading?" Jeff finally asked.

Garcia focused on his driving. He handed him the map when they reached the straight area on the switchback. "The jungles of La Joya. It's the prettiest place on earth."

CHAPTER 65

A S THE LITTLE pickup truck turned off the main road it pitched and groaned as it went over some very rough terrain. Jeff began to feel like a milkshake. "How on earth did you ever find this place?" Jeff was thankful the ground seemed to be leveling out. In the distance a waterfall came into view with the Gulf Coast in the background.

Garcia began to bubble with joy, "I knew you'd like this spot. When we were young, my father used to bring us on hunting trips here. Did your father ever take you hunting?"

"The only thing my father ever hunted was tail. Thankfully, I was never invited." Jeff laughed, but he could see that the joke was lost in translation. After a minute of explaining, Garcia laughed and Jeff continued, "My father left me when I was just a young boy. My mother fought for our survival and she did very well for us. We never had a lot, but I always had a roof over my head and food on the table. She was killed by my best friend and I still miss her." He shocked himself with this outpouring of emotion.

The very powerful words Garcia had just heard left

him speechless. He rolled the truck to a stop and got out. "I'm sorry Jeff," was all he managed to say.

Jeff sighed and took the conversation to a happier place. "Let's focus on the positive. This place is absolutely breathtaking. Has it changed much over the years?"

Garcia looked around toward the ledge of the waterfall and pointed to the rock. "The vegetation over there is much thicker this time of year. There seems to have been a mudslide over on that ledge. Besides that, it seems to have been untouched by time. Let's eat some lunch and if you're up for it we can take a little hike toward the falls. Are you feeling better?"

"I am feeling better, it must be all this mountain air." Jeff had to admit that this place seemed to be lifting his spirits.

They ate their lunch and drank some water. The food seemed to fill Jeff's body with energy. This could be the best he'd felt since the death of Emily and Sophia. The combination of antidepressants and a bellyful of food made him ready for a little adventure.

"Let's saddle up, partner." He told Garcia.

Together they headed for the waterfall in the distance, unaware of what they were about to discover.

CHAPTER 66

TRAVELING OVER THE terrain was like walking on a large sponge. He'd never seen this type of dense vegetation in his entire life. He understood why they couldn't go any further with the vehicle. This place would be a botanist's dream. Everywhere he looked, he saw another plant he'd never seen before. He finally turned to Garcia and said, "It seems like we are walking on a thousand years of roots and vegetation."

Garcia stopped, adjusted the rifle strap on his shoulder and turned to answer. "I've never thought about it that way. But, yes, this place keeps growing and growing. Unfortunately, as my father would say, this land has been fertilized with the blood of my ancestors. We were told this often on our hunting trips. In the 16th century the Spaniards killed my people and opened a military post not too far from here. They ruled with an iron fist for nearly three hundred years. Then the land was given back to us in the 1800's and we were given our independence. There is still the constant bickering and arguing of our people over what should be done with the land, not to mention whom actually owns it. For this reason, my father always took it upon himself to

hunt on any land with game to put food on his table."
Garcia stopped talking and pointed to a small brown
pheasant. "Jeff, look over there. This must be your lucky
day. There's a bearded wood-partridge. They are almost
extinct." He made a move for his rifle.

"You just said they were almost extinct. Why kill it?"
Jeff grabbed the barrel and stopped him from sighting
the pheasant.

"Because after I kill it and stuff it, I can say I have
one." Garcia looked somewhat annoyed with him. He
pulled the rifle barrel out of Jeff's hand, but the pheasant
was gone.

The words he'd just heard left him understanding
why endangered species became endangered. Jeff pleaded
with him. "Can we not kill anything today? Please? I just
want to enjoy this beautiful place and leave it the way I
found it."

The lust for blood he'd seen in Garcia's eyes
disappeared as quickly as it came. Garcia seemed to
remember that the trip was for Jeff's benefit. "I'm sorry
Jeff. I forgot you really aren't a hunter. I still want to
show you the view from the ledge over by the waterfall
and then we'll leave. Are you up for it?"

Jeff nodded and they continued their hike up to the
waterfall. As the terrain got steeper his pace lessened.
It was then decided that Jeff should take the lead with
Garcia and his rifle behind him. If Jeff were to lose his
footing, Garcia would be behind him to keep him safe.
When Jeff reached the top of the ledge and looked over to
the horizon beyond the Gulf Coast, he was overwhelmed
by its beauty. The sounds of the waterfall created the
most peaceful place on earth. He looked down over the

ledge to see a thirty-metre drop onto the rocks below. Best not to look down, he urged himself.

When Garcia reached his side he thanked him for bringing him to such a beautiful place. They both heard the voice at the same time. They were so busy admiring the captivating scenery that they failed to notice the small opening in the blocked cave. They turned to see a man's hand waving and a hoarse whisper shouting, "Help me!"

CHAPTER 67

GARCIA GROANED LOUDLY as he pushed on a large branch he'd retrieved from the forest floor. The result was the same as the last time. The branch snapped like a twig. Jeff thought out loud, "I may not have my strength, but I still have my brain. Your truck has a jack to change the tire, right?" Garcia already knew what he meant and left for the truck. Jeff saw the pair of eyes in the small opening dart in terror back and forth. Jeff did his best to explain to the man what they were planning on doing. "We're going to try to move the rock with a car jack."

Except for the initial call for help, the man had not been able to speak. Even if Jeff were able to see Calderone's entire face, he wouldn't recognize him. The man was a shadow of his former self. His face was withered and sunken from the rapid loss of fat and fluids. No sign of any recognition was shown on the part of Calderone. Either he truly didn't recognize Jeff, or he was completely gone, in some sort of delirious state of shock.

Garcia came back with the scissor jack and placed it in the eight-inch opening. The rock moved slowly as he cranked the handle on the jack. It seemed to protest, as it audibly groaned against the rock ledge. The opening went from eight inches to nine. Pebbles and dirt fell from above their heads. Garcia continued turning the jack's crank as sweat poured down into his eyes in the tropical heat. All of a sudden the screw portion of the jack broke with a loud snap as the metal pinged against the rock. "Dammit!" was all Garcia managed to say.

Jeff thought quickly about how the man came to be in the cave and asked Calderone, "How did you get here. Do you have a vehicle? Blink once for yes." Calderone blinked once. "Where is it?"

Calderone mustered up all his remaining strength and whispered, "He told me he hid it in the bush."

Jeff could tell they were losing him. Questions about what had happened would have to wait. "We've got to find that vehicle and another jack." From his vantage point he was able to scan the area. A glint of metal caught Jeff's eye roughly sixty yards to the left of Garcia's truck. He pointed in that direction and asked Garcia, "What's that over there?"

Garcia went to the area and found the black SUV that had been camouflaged by branches and dirt. Jeff heard the smash as Garcia broke into the vehicle to retrieve the heavy-duty jack. Jeff's eyes lit up when he returned with a jack twice the size of the old one. "Now we're talking."

The newer jack made short work of moving the large boulder. The men held their breath against the stench of death as they removed Calderone from the cave. Calderone didn't have the strength to talk, let alone stand up. Jeff asked Garcia, "Are you strong enough to carry him down yourself or should we send for help?" Garcia handed him the rifle and picked up Calderone in a piggyback fashion. Together they began the steep descent back to the truck.

Under the cover of a dense bush, Glaaj looked on with disappointment.

CHAPTER 68

GLAAJ BEGAN DOING mental back flips as he tried to update his plan to suit the new development. He sighted his .30-30 Winchester rifle and debated shooting his prisoner. If he were to shoot him and leave without being noticed Jeff and Garcia would be none the wiser. If he didn't shoot him now, he risked the chance that Calderone would survive to tell the tale of his capture and torture.

Deep down Glaaj still felt that if Jeff were to witness the death of Calderone it would benefit him spiritually. Glaaj steadied his rifle against the branch of a tree. The shot from this distance was roughly seventy yards. He didn't have to be an expert marksman at this distance, but just in case he aimed for the center of Calderone's back. He took a deep breath and let it out slowly. With his mind made up, he slowly pulled the trigger. The loud explosion from the barrel quieted the wildlife. A loud whomp broke the silence as the bullet entered Calderone's body.

The bullet tore through Calderone's back and ricocheted inside. The bullet exited with enough force to penetrate Garcia's back, it entered his body tearing the left ventricle of his heart. The two men tumbled down to the bottom of the slope, hitting the rocks below with a sickening crunch, as if a bag of coconuts had been dropped.

On the ledge, Jeff stared at the blood splatter on his hand and on the barrel of the rifle he carried. Instinct took over and he sighted the rifle in the general area from where the shot came. Through the smoke he could see movement. He chambered a round and quickly took the shot. The noise and kickback from the rifle caught him off guard and he stumbled and fell backwards against some rocks. He regained his composure and fired off another quick shot. There were cries of pain in the distance. Jeff wasn't sure if they were coming from the wounded men below or if he'd just shot their attacker. He urgently wanted to find out. As carefully and as quickly as he could, he made his way down to the bottom to check on Garcia and Calderone.

Jeff reached back into his memory of his high school first-aid training. He used two fingers to check for a pulse on the left side of Garcia's neck. But felt nothing. This couldn't be happening. Knowing that the man they were trying to help was near death to begin with; the fact that he had a large gaping hole in his chest meant that the man was certainly dead. Therefore, the screams in the distance must have been the shooter's, he concluded.

Cautiously, Jeff made his way through the forest in the direction of the gun blast.

CHAPTER 69

THE SOUNDS FROM the forest floor sounded like breaking glass to Jeff as he tried to move quietly with his rifle at the ready. The day had gone from total peace to total chaos in a very short time. Sweat dripped from his brow onto the butt of the rifle making the stock slippery. He did his best to regulate his breathing as he swept the rifle from left to right, covering his field of vision.

A very loud snap shattered the silence and scattered birds from the trees. Jeff quickly took cover behind a large box elder maple. Once he was calm enough to examine his surroundings, he noticed that he had stepped on the branch that had sent the birds flying. He worked up his nerve and looked for a familiar rock or tree to get his bearings again. He noticed Garcia's truck in the distance. He remembered that the shooter's position was roughly parallel to the truck.

The blood on the trunk of an avocado tree indicated that Jeff was in the right area. More importantly he'd hit the shooter with a very lucky shot. Cautiously, he approached a blood-splattered tree and he heard a soft moan. He spun around and saw the shooter laying face down on the ground. Jeff turned Glaaj over with his foot. His eyes were immediately drawn to the man's blood-soaked abdomen. The wound on his stomach oozed out blackish blood. When Jeff examined the man's face, his jaw nearly hit the forest floor. "What the hell is going on here?"

Staring back at Jeff, barely alive, was Armand, the man who had taken over for Luis as foreman, the man who had helped build his home, the man who had bounced Emily on his knee. He was a part of his family. He had considered him as a friend. He threw Garcia's rifle to the ground and quickly applied pressure to the wound; it didn't matter. All of the bleeding was internal. Armand opened his eyes and coughed out blood as he tried to speak, "Jeff, I did it all for you, to make you better. He suffered to make you better. Look in my pocket."

Keeping pressure on the bullet hole, Jeff looked in his pockets and eventually found an identification card for Calderone. Jeff asked him, "That was Calderone up there?"

Armand nodded.

"You tortured and killed him to avenge Emily and Sophia's deaths?" Jeff asked.

Armand nodded again. This time the pain from his injuries made him wince.

"Garcia is dead. Do you know that? Why, Armand? Why? Garcia is dead. How the hell am I going to explain this to Al and Maria?" Jeff grabbed a handful of Armand's shirt and shook him as he screamed.

"I didn't mean to. Tell them I am sorry." Armand coughed and moaned. The loss of blood, combined with organ damage, made his colour change rapidly.

Armand's throat seemed to expand as he struggled for air. Blood bubbled from his mouth as he drowned in his own bodily fluids. Jeff rolled him onto his side, but it was too late. He convulsed and thrashed wildly and then he was still.

Jeff crouched over the body and shook his dead friend by his shirt, yelling. "Dammit! Dammit!" Jeff knelt and threw his arms in the air. He then covered his eyes with his hands in confusion. The adrenaline had run its course. Tears of exhaustion and grief streamed down his cheeks.

CHAPTER 70

J EFF FELT LIKE a wave of debilitating despair was about to overcome him. He battled his emotions as he reached into the right pocket of his jean shorts. He found the one-tranquilizer pill he'd brought along in case of an emergency. This definitely constituted an emergency. He dry swallowed the pill and wished he had more. He walked away from Armand's body trying to physically separate himself from the situation. He needed time to think.

The height of the afternoon sun told Jeff that the time was roughly four o'clock. Lunch and the peace derived from it seemed like days ago. He headed for Garcia's pickup truck for water and the hopes of nutrition; he needed energy to cope with the disastrous event. He drank from the water cooler and only then realized just how thirsty he was. He ate leftover granola trail mix even though he didn't feel like eating. He fully understood that the brain and body needed fuel to work properly. After a moment's rest to help force his stomach to keep the contents down, he headed back to retrieve Armand's rifle. Jeff picked up the .30-30 Winchester rifle, aimed it toward the waterfall and fired off a round. He went back to the truck and placed the rifle in the cab. Next, he headed toward Garcia and Calderone's bodies.

As he headed in the direction of the waterfall, he thought of the peace and serenity of this place; now for him it was shattered forever. If he never set foot in these parts again, he would die happy. Every instinct in his body was telling him to run. To run back to the safety of his mother's house, to forget these people, to forget the day's events, to forget everything.

The first thing that struck him when he saw Garcia's body again was the expression frozen on his face. It was an anguished face with open eyes. Garcia was bent over backwards on a large rock with his arms dangling toward the ground. Calderone lay in a fetal position in a crevasse behind a large boulder. The first thing Jeff decided to do was to fish the keys out of his brother-in-law's front right pocket. Flies flew off of the dead bodies and landed on his skin. The smell of death hit him hard as he dug his hand into the urine-soaked pocket. Garcia's body had evacuated itself, like all human beings when they die. He gagged hard three times and vomited. So much for his nutrition intake he so vitally needed.

Jeff estimated Garcia weighed about roughly one hundred and seventy pounds. He grabbed a hold of his left arm and the cuff of his shorts and pulled his body off the rock. Garcia landed on the ground with a thud as flies scattered everywhere. Instinctively Jeff said, "Sorry, Garcia." He waved the flies away from his face and pulled Garcia's torso up by the right arm and hooked his own arm through Garcia's feces and urine-soaked crotch. He hoisted him onto his shoulders in a fireman's carry.

Jeff took the first few tentative steps toward the truck

that was more than two hundred yards away. It might as well have been a thousand miles. The smells coming off of Garcia's body were too much for him to handle and his overall weakness was impeding him. The exercise he had done in the last several weeks was not enough to prepare for a dead man lift. He let the body slide off his shoulders and crash to the ground. "Fuck!" Jeff screamed so loud that birds shot from the trees. He wanted to turn around and kick Garcia in frustration.

There was no other way, he had to go and get help. He marched back to the truck fueled by his frustrations. He climbed behind the driver's seat, but when he tried to put the key in the ignition it wouldn't fit. He looked at the key and noticed that it had been bent when Garcia's body had hit the rocks. Painstakingly, he searched for a fist-sized rock. When he found one he lay the key on the truck box and tapped it gently flat. As he inserted the key into the ignition, he said a little prayer in his head, turned it and the engine roared. He turned on the headlights to blot out the fast approaching nightfall.

CHAPTER 71

J EFF ASSESSED HIS day on the drive back to Zempoala. Yes, it had been a bad day. Not as bad as Garcia and Armand's though, he felt sorry for them. Calderone was different. (Jeff felt Calderone had got what was coming to him). None of this would have ever happened if Calderone had accepted defeat that day and drove away carefully. Instead, the man had run over his beloved Sophia and little Emily.

Jeff drove the pickup truck back to the farm and parked out back. He climbed up the creaky back porch stairs and entered the kitchen area. He suddenly felt very sad for the Martinez family. They would have been far better off if he had never come into their lives.

Maria saw Jeff enter and immediately grew excited. "Al, come in here. Jeff and Garcia are finally back. Is Garcia getting the rest of his things from the truck?"

"Well, how was it?" Al entered the room.

Jeff remained silent. He didn't know where to start.

"He's dead, isn't he?" Everyone was shocked when, from the corner of the room, Jesus uttered those ominous words.

"You shouldn't say such things. That's not even

remotely funny." Al and Maria both thought that their son was being his usual morbid self.

Al noticed the look on Jeff's face, "Jeff, sit down. Tell us what has happened. Maria, you come sit too. Come sit down dear." Maria and Jeff both sat down. Jeff began to cry. Al rubbed his back anxious to hear what had happened.

Jeff began to try and explain the day's events. He told them about finding the man trapped in a cave. How they struggled with moving the stone at the waterfall and finally rescued him only to have a gunman shoot him. That man, he later found out, was Calderone. That was when Jeff changed the story to absolve himself of accidentally shooting Armand.

Jeff cleared his throat and continued, "Garcia returned fire in the direction of the gunman. It all happened so fast. I thought he'd crouch down for cover; but he was shot dead before he fell. He tumbled to the rocks below with Calderone. After checking on Garcia, I went to see who had shot at us, it turned out to be Armand. He told me about capturing Calderone for revenge. When I told him about Garcia being dead as well, he cried, he said he was sorry and then he died."

Maria started screaming. Al instructed Jesus to take her over to the couch. Jeff continued, "All three of them are dead in the forest. I tried to bring Garcia back but I was too weak." Jeff broke down and cried with his head on the table.

Al jumped up and the chair shot across the room. He paced in anger; trying to piece together everything he had just heard. It was late in the evening and he barked out orders to his son who was consoling Maria. "Jesus, get Lucky and the flashlights. We'll need the large brown tarp as well. Maria, I need you to be strong." He kissed Maria on the forehead as she lay on the couch in shock.

Al and Jesus came back into the kitchen just before they were about to leave and grabbed Jeff by each arm. "Jeff, you've got to come with us and show us where they are."

Jeff felt like lying in bed for another month after the day's tragic events, or maybe an endless swim was in order. The last thing he wanted to do was go back to that horrible place. He knew that the request was non-negotiable. "I just need to go back home first to get my medication." Wearily he rose from the table and left.

CHAPTER 72

THE RIDE BACK to La Joya was filled with tension. When there wasn't excruciating silence, there were deep probing questions from Al and Jesus. Jeff kept his spirits positive with the notion of his imminent departure from Mexico. As soon as he felt up to a long drive he would make arrangements to head back to Junction City.

Al continued with more questions, "It all makes no sense to me. Why would Armand shoot at Garcia? I could see why Garcia would fire back if he felt he was under attack. He was always an excellent marksman. It makes sense that he made the shot. Especially not knowing who the attacker was, but if Calderone was already shot dead why would he keep shooting?"

"Maybe Armand snapped after the death of Sophia and Emily. We were all grieving. Maybe instead of grieving he was plotting his revenge." Jeff did his best to try and fill in the holes.

Jesus, who had been silent for much of the car ride, finally spoke with an edge in his voice. "Maybe you are bending the truth Jeff? There might be something you are leaving out. Something that may make you look bad. Maybe you killed them?"

"If I was trying to cover something up, I never would have told you anything. I would have placed a rifle in each mans hands and left them for someone else to find them." Jeff protested immediately and felt on the edge of another breakdown. He had taken double the dose of his medication, which helped, but it made the top of his head feel like it was swelling.

"Enough! There has been enough for one day. We're almost there." Al quieted them both.

The next fifteen minutes of the drive was spent in silence.

"Slow down, it's coming up ahead on your left. Turn right here." Jeff gave the directions when they drew closer to the place.

"I haven't been here in more than ten years. I used to bring the boys here on hunting trips." Al reminisced as he recognized his surroundings. Sadness struck him as he realized 'the boys' was now just Jesus.

"That was what Garcia told me all about today. He loved those times with you. I'm so sorry Al." Jeff said.

After several tense moments driving over the rough terrain in the dark and lighting the area with a spotlight, they finally came to the spot next to Armand's body. Jeff directed the spotlight to guide Jesus and Al over to Armand's body. He kept the light on their path as they carried Armand back toward the pickup truck. He could hear Al and Jesus curse as they stumbled and dropped the body. The stench from the corpse was too much for them to handle. They trudged on and placed Armand in the back of the pickup.

Jeff was amazed at the two mens' resolve to take care of the situation themselves. He thought of that horrific day when Emily and Sophia had died in the clinic. Dr. Wolfe had informed them of a $45 fee for submitting a government death certificate. The poor people of Mexico didn't bother with forms; they just took care of the situation and buried their own dead. You could die in the morning and buried by the evening. There would be no police investigation. A crime scene investigation team would not show up to piece together the story. Armand and Garcia would be buried on the hill with the rest of their ancestors.

Al and Jesus' eyes streamed tears onto their cheeks as they carried Garcia's body back to the pickup. Again Jeff lit their path with the spotlight. They gently deposited the body into the truck next to Armand. Al spoke to Jeff through his exhaustion. "Are you able to walk us over to where Calderone's body is located?"

Jeff nodded and said, "Yeah, it's about forty yards to the left of where you found Garcia." He stepped out of the truck and with shaky legs walked over to Calderone's body.

Jesus still regarded Jeff with mistrust. He continued to speak to Jeff with an edge in his voice. "Come and help me pull Calderone out from behind this rock. My father has done enough for one day." His body language was very aggressive.

Jeff could tell by Jesus' expression that he wished Jeff were lying dead in the back of the pickup. He finally snapped and spoke to Jesus. "Look at me!" Jesus looked at him with daggers in his eyes. "I wish it were me in the back of that truck, but it's not. Take a look at the rifles when you get home. You'll know I am telling you the truth. Both of those rifles were fired twice. Just like I said." Jesus stared at him blankly. "Better yet, go over to where Armand's body was found and you'll see the shell casings; just like I said."

Jesus seemed to soften up from the confrontation. "Let's just get the body back. I am too full of anger and sorrow to think straight." With great difficulty Jeff and Jesus carried Calderone to the truck. The job was not difficult because he was heavy (in fact you could count the ribs on his body) or because Calderone was curled in a ball and in full rigour mortis. The job was difficult because of the smell from the body that made them gag and twist their faces away. They dared not open their mouths to talk. The risk of inviting hundreds of excited flies buzzing from the body into their mouths was too great.

The ride back to the farm was an experience Jeff never wanted to relive. It was a long drive in total silence, surrounded by sorrow-filled men. When the truck slowed, the air in the truck cab filled with the smell of death from the three bodies.

CHAPTER 73

JEFF HAD NEARLY passed out from exhaustion when they had arrived with the bodies late the previous night. He was sent to bed as soon as the men returned. His night was anything but peaceful. Once his head hit the pillow it became filled with nightmare images of death from his past. Cory came back as the conductor of a strange dead orchestra. The music they played was as grotesque as their rotting corpses. The orchestra pit contained dusty books lit by candles held in human skulls. Garcia and Armand's rotting bodies took their seats in two of the three empty chairs. They picked up their instruments, Garcia played a piccolo and Armand played the violin. Suddenly everyone stopped playing and pointed to Jeff to take the third remaining seat. He adamantly refused and the orchestra of the dead leapt at him with incredible speed. He ran until his legs tired and he fell to the ground with a bone rattling crash. He came out of the dream as the orchestra of the dead pulled on his limbs causing excruciating pain. The dream seemed to have lasted all night. When he opened his eyes, the sun blinded his vision and his arms and legs felt numb.

The morning heat made the smallest task seem daunting. Jeff stood in front of the two open pine coffins in a trance-like state as sweat trickled down his ribs. Garcia and Armand's bloody clothing had been replaced with plain white cotton robes. Their eyes were covered with five peso coins. Dust rose up from the group of relatives who pounded the ground with their fists in anger. The men stood in the background as the women consoled and hugged each other.

Jeff's van was already packed and ready for the drive back to Junction City. In some respects he was mentally already on his way. He did everything in his power to stay in control of his emotions.

Jeff approached Al who stood with his head hung low in mourning. Jeff leaned over and gave his condolences. Al clasped his hand and whispered, "Thank you." He then added, "Jeff, I forgive you and I understand why you have to leave. Always know that you are welcome to come and visit us whenever you can. With your leaving here today I have lost two sons." Al released his hand.

Jeff grabbed him and gave him a big hug, "Thank you. You'll always be like a father to me." Jeff's curiosity got the better of him and he asked, "What did you do with Calderone?"

Al motioned with his eyes in the direction of the offal pit near the back of the property. Jeff remembered the first tour he had received of the property. It all seemed like a lifetime ago. He had been warned about the deep offal pit that contained the carcasses of animals that had succumbed to the elements. It contained powerful bacteria and maggots which feasted on animal waste and now, apparently, Calderone's body.

"He will help keep the grass green." Al simply nodded his head.

In Jeff's private meeting with Maria and Al, he told them how he would always love and appreciate them as parents and how he would miss them both. He handed Al the keys to his home and told him, "Enjoy it. Mi casa, su casa." My home is your home. As he passed the others, he made his good-byes to each one of them with promises of his return someday. Deep down he knew he would never come back to this place.

Jeff pulled out his maps and planned his route back to Junction City. As he entered the van the afternoon heat made the inside feel like a sauna. The van had survived well in storage because he had kept the engine tuned over the years. He listened to the happy noises of the engine from under the hood as his proof of his mechanical skills. It seemed like deja vu as he drove with what remained of his stolen cash hidden in the van's floor. He stopped in Ciudad de Mexico to eat at Mama Rosa's Condesa. He ordered some food and a cerveza at the bar. After the bartender left to place his order, Jeff's eyes were drawn to the television behind him. A pretty woman stood with her two lovely children and she pleaded for help into the camera. "Veronica Calderone" was the caption below the image on the television. Tears streamed down her cheeks as she pleaded for information about the disappearance of her husband.

Jeff asked the bartender to put his meal in a paper bag when he returned with his hot plate of food. As the bartender transferred his meal to a brown bag, Jeff thought about Calderone's decomposed body in the offal pit. He shuddered at the thought. Jeff thanked the bartender, grabbed his meal and left the bar. He felt a sudden urgency to place his feet back on U.S. soil.

CHAPTER 74

SWEAT BEADED ON Jeff's brow because of the springtime heat as he approached the United States border patrol booth. He second-guessed his decision to cross the border with his expired American passport. What if his name was flagged for attempted murder in Junction City? What if they found the safe compartment behind the rear bumper with the double locks? What if they questioned him about his whereabouts for the last five years? What if his very simple plan didn't work?

Two more vehicles were ahead of him, waiting to go through the border patrol. He took several deep breaths and prepared himself. He rolled down his window and gave the pretty faced, overweight, middle-aged border patrol agent his best Tom Cruise smile. Little did he know that most people now considered Tom Cruise to be completely insane. He relaxed when she smiled back. Luck was apparently on his side today. Jeff handed her his American passport. "How are you today?" he asked.

Jeff was thrown when her demeanor changed from polite to authoritative and businesslike. "Citizenship?"

"American." Jeff replied.

"Where are you headed?" she asked.

"Home to Junction City." Jeff replied. He didn't like the way she had started eyeballing him suspiciously.

Then it happened.

Two cars back, several chicken crates had toppled onto the ground and broken open. Chickens ran loose. They ran around a farmer's old tan truck as they made their great escape. The farmer rushed out of his truck and tried to corral the chickens as feathers flew through the air. His attempts were unsuccessful. It was almost like he pushed the birds instead of grabbing them. This sort of commotion was unacceptable at the border crossing. Guards immediately appeared out of nowhere to assist the man and berate him for his unsafe load.

The border patrol guard serving Jeff watched the comedic event unfold with a scowl on her face. After several seconds she seemed to remember she was in the process of serving an American citizen. "Sorry. Looks like it's going to be one of those days. I hate days like this. They only get weirder. Welcome back, Mr. Brooks. Have a safe drive back to Junction City." She waved goodbye to Jeff as she handed him back his passport.

Jeff pounded on the steering wheel as he shouted with excitement after clearing the border. Getting through safely gave him the greatest high of his life. He couldn't believe his simple distraction plan had worked flawlessly. Back about fifteen miles, at a rest stop area, Jeff had met a skinny, short Mexican farmer named Juan and his load of chickens. Jeff immediately hammered out a deal with the man for the sale of all his chickens. The man almost fell off the bench when Jeff told him he could keep all the chickens afterwards. The man agreed, why wouldn't he? After giving him one hundred dollars, Jeff explained that if he followed his instructions at the border crossing, another one hundred dollars would be sent to him in the mail. Juan surprised Jeff when he told him that the other hundred dollars should be sent to his sister Lolita in Las Cruses, New Mexico. He explained to Jeff that his sister's son needed an operation and she was struggling to make ends meet as a chambermaid. Juan had willingly toppled over the crate of chickens twenty seconds after Jeff handed over his passport.

The I-35 stretched for miles into the heart of Texas toward San Antonio. Jeff found a post office just outside the city. He pulled out his luggage and reached into the secret compartment for some traveling cash. Inside of the van, he counted out 61 hundred-dollar bills. He wrote a quick note on the inside of the envelope.

Dear Lolita,

Your brother Juan helped me out today and told me of your struggles. Please pay Juan his $100.00 next time when you see him. The $6,000.00 is for you and your son. I hope this helps.

Jeff

Jeff felt good about himself as he sent the registered package to Lolita.

CHAPTER 75

THE AFTERNOON HEAT began to dissipate, as did Jeff's adrenaline rush. He decided to check into the finest hotel money could buy. He had no idea what awaited him when he returned to Junction City. The possibility of contact with his dead mother far outweighed the dangers of incarceration.

Jeff took the Oak Lawn Ave. exit off I-35 and pulled into the Warwick Melrose Hotel. He pulled into the valet parking area and paid an extra large tip to make sure the rear of the van was parked against a wall. Rich people expect a certain level of security. The lobby looked like a palace, complete with a large chandelier, which hung in the entrance, marble mosaic on the floor, tile mosaic on the ceiling and painted colonial woodwork that reminded Jeff of his home in Zempoala. Unlike his home though, some tasteless person had painted over the beautiful wood floors and pillars.

Jeff approached the check-in desk where an elegant man stood at attention in a three-piece suit. His nametag said Bradley, "Welcome to The Warwick, sir. How can I help you?"

Jeff was dressed in brown khaki shorts, light white

cotton shirt, deck shoes and no socks. He definitely did not feel like a 'sir'.

"I'm traveling on my way to Kansas and would like a room." Jeff cleared his throat.

Bradley the service clerk politely scanned his attire and asked, "How will you be paying for that sir?"

"Cash." Jeff smiled.

"Excellent, I have a corner king room available in the south west corner with a beautiful view of the city. Total will come to $314.27. I'll need your driver's license and a major credit card please." Bradley responded.

Jeff reached for his wallet and thought how strange it was to be back on U.S. soil. He didn't even carry his wallet when he was in Mexico. A wave of pain hit him when he saw a little girl the same age as Emily run through the lobby with her mom in hot pursuit behind her. The giggling echoed in the lobby. He quietly mourned the loss of his family as he stared blankly into the adjacent office.

"Sir, is there a problem?" Bradley cleared his throat.

Jeff composed himself and handed over $400.00 in cash, his license and a credit card. "No problem just tired."

"Sir, your credit card has expired, last year." Bradley whispered to conceal the possibility of embarrassment for Jeff as he handed him back his credit card.

Without skipping a beat Jeff took the card, examined it and wrapped another hundred-dollar bill around the same card and handed it back. "I've been meaning to get that renewed. I'm sure this one will be fine and we'll just call it even."

"We certainly can, sir. If there is any other way I can

make your stay more pleasurable do not hesitate to ask for Bradley at the front desk." Bradley smiled at the large tip.

He took the elevator up to the fifth floor and walked into the corner king room. The room was the same as the lobby with its lavish colonial molding and attention to detail. Jeff still wondered why anyone would paint over expensive hardwood. After a long hot shower, he changed into a plush bathrobe and sat down at a small table. He savoured every bite of his thick T-bone steak and potato supper ordered from the room service menu. After eating, he lay on the bed in complete silence for a while and then called Michael in Junction City. His mood brightened at the sound of Michael's voice, "I can't tell you how good it is to hear your voice."

"Ditto. Where are you man?" Michael was equally pleased.

Jeff went through all the small talk about his home in Junction City and Michael's life. He took his time and finally got through the tear filled, gut wrenching tales of the death of his family, he explained how he crossed the border and reached Dallas.

Jeff continued. "Michael, I'd like you to do me a favour before I get there. I want you to call Chief Mullen to let him know I'll be home by tomorrow evening. Let him know that I am willing to admit to everything that happened with Cory." Silence on the line, "Are you still there?"

"Yeah, are you sure about this?" Michael was stunned.

Jeff had had plenty of time to think on his long drive to Dallas. That was when he had realized that Michael was the closest friend he had left. If he couldn't live at home, he didn't want to live.

"Yeah, I'm sure." Jeff replied.

CHAPTER 76

THE YOUTHFUL VALET exited the vehicle and handed the keys to Jeff. Jeff wondered what the young man would say if he knew the value of the van. Oh, she doesn't look like much, but look under her floorboard and she's worth more than $400,000. Jeff tipped the valet $20, drove out of the Warwick Grand driveway and turned the van west toward the I-35 on-ramp.

The early morning start was needed for the long drive ahead. He pulled into the Oklahoma IHOP after driving for a little more than two hours. He sat down at a window booth with a direct line of sight to the van. A perky brunette came and took his order and quickly left. There was no time for her to chat in the hurried pace of American fast food.

Jeff continued his journey home on the I-35. He was surprised by how little had changed. Sure, there was new construction, but basically things had remained unchanged. The long drive had him thinking about the possibility of communicating with his mother. Could her spirit really be playing host in his home? He and Michael had danced around the topic over the phone. Really, it required more of a face-to-face conversation.

Jeff pulled off again in Wichita for the best wood-oven pizza in the world. He salivated as he thought about it. It had been more than six years since he'd last had it. The van seemed to remember the way as he exited off at the E Kellogg Ave. exit and headed over to Il Vicino Wood Oven Pizza, 4817 E Douglas Ave. Jeff's tongue tingled as he turned the corner and saw that the restaurant was still there.

Jeff sat down at the table and ordered a calzone before the waiter could even say hello. He also ordered four more to go, Michael would thank him. He drank a Rolling Rock beer as he ate and his brain began to come around to all the things he loved about being back in the U.S. The food made both his belly and mind happy. He left a generous tip and headed to the washroom before he left. In the washroom stall, he read a very funny comic on the back of the door. It was a drawing of two nuclear physicists hard at work. A third one came out from a washroom door and the caption below said, "Do not go in there. I've just ejected my toxic spent fuel rods." He looked forward to the last leg of the trip.

It always seemed like the last hours of a trip home were the longest. Jeff was disappointed that there wasn't really anything new during the drive.

"Well, look at that." He said, pleasantly surprised. After not speaking for so long, the sound of his own voice seemed to give him a bit of a shock. Nevertheless there it was, something new. It was a 30-ton monument that announced the arrival to the Flint Hills area. The monument stood nine feet tall and twenty-five feet long. It must have cost a fortune.

He decided to take the I-335 to the I-70 and come in

the back way to Junction City. Why go through Kansas City if he didn't have to? Jeff started to really think about his future and his freedom. Would Chief Mullen be waiting there with handcuffs? How much jail time would he do? He was willing to do the time for his freedom. He passed the sign announcing, *Welcome to Junction City, population 18,886.*

Jeff pulled into the driveway of his childhood home at around nine thirty in the evening. There were no police cars waiting for him. He could see a light on in the living room and blue flashes from a television. He stepped out of the van with the calzones in hand and walked in the front door.

Michael jumped up as if he had been shot out of a cannon. Jeff was surprised that a man of his size could move that fast.

"Jesus, you scared the hell out of me. Thank God. You're back safe though. How was your drive?" He was almost shouting.

Jeff thought his friend looked tired. He noticed Michael kept glancing back toward the La-Z-Boy chair.

"The drive went really well. I saw a huge monument for Flint Hills." Jeff replied as he scanned the room.

"Yeah, I saw that on the news the other day. I spoke to Mullen for you and he says that you can go down to the station in the morning and speak to him whenever you get a chance. He didn't sound too concerned." Michael laughed.

Jeff was pleased to hear that. "That's good news. Tell me about this guy who told you about my mom's spirit?" Before Michael could answer his question, he pointed in the direction of the shotgun propped up against the wall.

"What's with the shotgun?" Jeff sighed, he noticed the shotgun propped against the wall.

"I'll explain. Let's sit down." Michael sighed.

Michael drank and ate calzones as he spent the next two hours telling Jeff of the strange occurrences over the last several months. Fear had gripped him so tightly that he had armed himself. Michael continued, "These calzones are fabulous. Jack wants to come over and help us out with your mother's spirit. He says she is very easy to communicate with."

Jeff, understandably, was overwhelmed with the amount of information. He scanned the room for any sort of signs from his mother.

"Let me sleep on it and we'll figure it all out after I see Chief Mullen in the morning." He replied sleepily.

He cried himself to sleep as he grieved the loss of his wife and daughter. The only silver lining was that he was finally back where he belonged.

CHAPTER 77

JEFF WOKE UP to birds singing the praises of springtime just outside his window. The rising sun illuminated the dew that covered the grass. It was good to be home after his long drive yesterday, but he was still tired. He hoped meeting with Chief Mullen today would alleviate his anxiety.

Jeff came out of the bedroom to find Michael standing with his coffee on the beige linoleum floor in the kitchen. He wore plaid boxers and a blue T-shirt with a voluptuous blonde giving two thumbs up on the front. Michael's large stomach stretched out the blonde's figure quite nicely. Michael seemed too sleepy to notice his friend of more than twenty years enter the kitchen as he stared at the china set out on the table.

Jeff cleared his throat before he spoke. "I think we should put those dishes away."

Michael almost jumped out of his skin. "Jesus! You scared the hell out of me." He thought about Jeff's comment and replied, "I'm not doing it. You put them away and they'll be back on the table tomorrow."

Jeff stared at him in disbelief. Clearly Michael was rattled by the whole poltergeist situation. Jeff remained doubtful. Still he felt it was better to allow some time to pass before he addressed the possibility of his mother's ghost. "Let's head out for breakfast like old times. We won't worry about the dishes right now. I'm sure Mama's Diner is still doing a brisk business."

"You'll be happy to know that not much has changed around here." Michael nodded.

Indeed not much had changed. The diner still had the same familiar faces in it. Most faces were a little older, yet they all took notice of Jeff as he walked in the door. There were hugs and back slaps all around. After they finished the greasy breakfasts that sat in their stomachs like muddy gravel, Michael asked him about his meeting. "What are you planning on telling Chief Mullen?"

"I plan on telling him everything. The truth, the whole truth and nothing but the truth." Jeff chuckled.

"Everything? Cory? The bank job?" Michael looked to his friend in disbelief.

Jeff cut him off with a wave of his hand and put a finger to his lips.

"Shush! Of course I'm not telling him about the bank job. Just everything that happened with Cory, the reason I had to leave this place, the reasons I want to come back and stay. It feels like I've been running for five years now. I don't want to run any more." Jeff put a twenty on the table and the two of them got up and left.

Jeff's palms began to sweat as he walked up the (Junction City Police Department's) front steps. Just like Michael had said, not much had changed. He walked in and headed for the reception desk where he spoke to a familiar looking officer. He read the nametag. It said Constable David Hill. Jeff took a deep breath. Were these going to be his last moments of freedom? "Hello. My name is Jeff Brooks. I am here to speak with Chief Mullen."

Chapter 78

J EFF SAT IN a small white room on a heavy grey metal chair. He surmised that the weight of the chair would make it difficult to throw or use as a weapon. For the last ten minutes he had waited patiently for the Chief. Time had no meaning anymore. He imagined himself sitting in a six foot by ten-foot prison cell for at least ten hours a day for the next couple of years and shuddered.

The jovial Chief Mullen opened the door, breaking Jeff's train of thought. He smiled at Jeff like a long lost son. "Jeff Brooks, it's been a long time. How long has it been? Where have you been? It's good to see you again."

Jeff felt tears well up in his eyes. About seven years ago Chief Mullen had broke the news to Jeff at his work when his mother had died. The Chief had been shaken-up after being one of the first on the scene. Jeff looked at the imposing muscular man and remembered the day he had given him a comforting hug after the terrible news. The Chief had aged well. His snug uniform displayed a fit body that was well taken care of.

Jeff felt a lump grow in his throat and wondered if he would be able to talk. He swallowed hard and began.

"Chief, it's good to see you too. It's been at least six years, maybe seven. You look as fit as ever."

The Chief took the compliment in stride and continued, "Thanks. You only get one life. You only get one body. Most people treat their personal property better than they do themselves. It's a damn shame."

The friendly conversation made Jeff feel at ease. "Chief, I came down here today to confess what happened the day Cory died." Jeff stared into Chief Mullen's eyes.

The Chief's facial expression changed to concern. "Let me go and get a pad of paper and a pen." He stood up and left the interview room door open. It took all of Jeff's courage not to bolt out the door.

The Chief returned with a pen and paper in hand. Jeff continued, "Chief Mullen, two days before Cory Blake died, I went over to his house to speak to him because he and I had gotten into an argument the night before in a bar. When I got over to the Blake house, Peggy was there and Cory wasn't. Since we were little kids, if Cory was upset or in trouble, he would climb up the trees at his parents place and wait until he felt it was safe to come back down. That day I went over to see him and I saw a pantry up in the tree. I climbed up and opened it to find . . . " Jeff felt very emotional.

Chief Mullen already knew of the pantry found on the Blake property by the F.B.I. In it they found evidence from the murders of Jeff's fiancé, his mother, his friend Chris, his brother-in-law Frank and the auto-body shop owner, jars of spent bullets and jars of fingernails. Everything had been itemized and labeled. The story of the killings had rocked Junction City. Chief Mullen nodded, "I know, Jeff. We found it too."

Jeff dried his eyes and continued, "After I found the pantry, I realized that my closest friend was a monster. I had to know why. I know it was wrong not to come to the police right away, but something inside me snapped." Jeff took a sip from a glass of water that seemed to have appeared from nowhere.

The Chief looked at Jeff as he drank and wondered what he would have done in the same situation. Would his badge have been enough of a shield to stop himself from crossing over the thin blue line of justice and revenge?

Jeff set the cup back on the table and started from where he'd left off. "That's when I came up with the idea to get Cory to tell me the truth. I know what I did was wrong and that is why I am here today. In my garage the following day, when Cory came over to meet me, I hit him with my axe in his lower back. I wanted to keep him from ever killing anyone else. I also wanted to know the truth. Why did he kill everyone that mattered to me?" Jeff took another sip. He felt good about finally getting all of this off his chest. He felt like the large elephant he'd been carrying on his shoulders had finally moved on. "So I bandaged the wound in his back and waited until he woke up again. Then he told me that he had been hearing voices since he was young. Voices had told him about all sorts of conspiracies. He had become so attached to me that I was his only reason for living. I felt sorry for him. We'd been friends since we were six." Tears began to flow freely down Jeff's cheeks.

The Chief had heard many sad stories in this room, but none sadder than this. He rubbed Jeff's shoulder and handed him a tissue to wipe his eyes.

Jeff took the tissue and said, "Thanks Chief. After Cory told me all this, I drove him to the hospital. Cory started to freak out while I was driving. He pulled out a gun from his bag. I had been through his bag when he was unconscious and removed the bullets. I wanted to know if he would use the gun on me. He pulled it out and fired it at me. I was shocked to see how mentally far gone he was. I told him I was taking him to the hospital and they were going to get him some help. Cory told me that if I tried, he was going to tell people he was going to shoot them with the gun. I tried to take the gun from his hand when we arrived at the hospital and that's when I noticed that he'd super glued the gun to it. I was so frustrated that I put him on the bench outside the Geary Hospital. I didn't know what else to do. I thought I'd taken all the bullets, but after I came back from calling the F.B.I. to let them know I'd found Cory, he'd chambered a round in the gun and pointed it at me. I was so depressed that I told him to go ahead and shoot. He didn't and I drove away." Jeff broke down in tears.

CHAPTER 79

JUST WHEN CHIEF Mullen thought the saddest story in the world was over, Jeff told him about his new life in Mexico. He explained how his pregnant wife and daughter had been run down and killed in Zempoala.

Mullen waited until Jeff composed himself and then finally spoke. "Jeff, I am truly sorry for all that you have been through. I sincerely hope that you'll never see that kind of suffering again in your lifetime. As to your admission of guilt in the death of Cory Blake, the State of Kansas stipulates that in the event of aggravated assault, charges must be raised within two years. From your admissions here today, you did assault Cory and you did break the law, but the statute of limitation on aggravated assault has passed. So even if I wanted to charge you, which I don't, I couldn't within the letter of the law."

Jeff was relieved to find out that the information he had read on the Internet was true. When he was at the Warwick Melrose Hotel, he had googled the statute of limitations on aggravated assault to find out what sort of trouble he would be in when he reached Junction City. For that reason he had lied about gluing the gun to Cory's hand and giving him one bullet.

The Chief continued, "Since Cory had glued the gun to his own hand, that means that you weren't directly or indirectly responsible for his death. The same goes for the bullet. If you knowingly gave a suicidal man a loaded gun and he got himself killed, then you could be held responsible for manslaughter. That depends, of course, on how good the lawyer of the accused person is." Chief Mullen looked down at his notes in amazement.

Jeff's emotions were about to explode like a volcano. Chief Mullen had just inadvertently confirmed his suspicions. If Jeff had not changed the details about the glued gun and the bullet, he would have been charged with manslaughter instead of a casual walk out the precinct door. The statute of limitations for manslaughter was ten years, not two years like aggravated assault.

Chief Mullen looked up from his notes and said, "I have a few phone numbers I'd like you to call Jeff. When a person has been through these kinds of traumatic events, it's important to speak to someone. I am proud to say that Junction City now has a couple of the finest grief counselors available who would be happy to help you through these emotional times."

Jeff blotted the tears from his eyes. He knew the Chief was right. "Any help you could give me would be much appreciated, Chief. It felt really good finally telling you everything. It is like a great weight has been lifted from my shoulders." Jeff sighed and then continued. "Chief, I wanted to get your opinion on something. Do you believe in ghosts?"

Chief Mullen looked at him with amusement in his eyes. "As a matter of fact I do. Most of the staff here is convinced that the station is haunted. That being said, it also means that there has been many a good practical joke played on one another. Fishing lines set up as trip wires to make a stack of papers fall when a person enters the room. They bang pipes and moan in the night. It's hard to know where the real haunts start and where the pranks end. Often it is when I'm alone in the office late. Why do you ask?"

Jeff nodded and tilted his head sideways, "Michael is convinced that my mother is haunting the house. Says he has a friend who came over and said she needed to speak to me. I'm not sure what to believe. I figure that if this guy wants money then it probably isn't true."

Jeff and Chief Mullen shook hands and Jeff thanked him for all his help. He left the police station a thousand pounds lighter, and a free man.

CHAPTER 80

ICHAEL AND JEFF sat in blue and white deck chairs as they soaked in the springtime sun. Iced mugs kept their beer crystallized along the edges. As the beer hit Jeff's lips he felt that his life might finally be back to normal. Nirvana blasted through the open kitchen windows onto the deck where they sat outside. The springtime air filled his head with the prospect of better times ahead.

Jeff turned to Michael and shouted over the music. "I've been thinking of buying a cottage outside of Milford state park. It's close enough that you could stop by every weekend and we could do some great fishing up there. Maybe water-skiing, Seadoo, or sailing, what do you think?" Jeff smiled and gulped more beer. He desperately searched for something that would give immediate gratification back to his miserable existence.

Michael stopped drinking his beer in mid-sip. "You're offering me a free cottage to use whenever I'd like? Party with my closest friend, as often as I can make it over to Milford Lake, which is like paradise? I'd say that you're a bonafide freakin' genius. Good to have you back man." They clinked mugs and nodded cheers.

Jeff spoke of the other matter that had hung over their heads since his return. He had kept a close eye on certain objects in the home he felt his mother might still cherish. He'd seen nothing, felt nothing and heard, nothing strange or paranormal in the house. Personally, he felt that Michael must have smoked some weed laced with a bit of PCP. He looked over at Michael and said, "So this guy Jack, you're convinced that he is for real?"

This had grown into a very touchy subject over the last several days. Michael shook his head up and down vehemently, "I'm telling you, Jack told me things about your mom that only she would know. If you had been here when the dishes smashed on the ground and the china set kept reappearing, we wouldn't be having this conversation." Michael took a long gulp from his mug.

Jeff felt bad for his friend. The last thing he wanted was to make him feel foolish. "All right, you've convinced me. Call Jack and set up a meeting with him. If he wants money or anything like that, then tell him not to bother coming over."

Michael grabbed the cordless phone and walked away from the deck and the music. He called Jack and spent several moments nodding his head as he gestured with his free hand. He walked back to the deck and sat down. "He is going to come over tonight and says he doesn't want any money. He says that you won't be disappointed."

Jeff grabbed another frozen mug from the freezer in the kitchen and poured another frosty beer. He aimlessly stared around at the china set and the various knick-knacks his mother used to cherish. The skeptic in him drank his beer and shook his head in denial. The optimist in him longed to speak to his mom.

CHAPTER 81

JEFF STOOD AT attention in front of the open barbeque as the late evening sun lit up the sky in brilliant purple and pink. The blood on the steaks began to pool with the melted butter, this indicated the perfect time to flip them. His mother had explained to him how to cook steaks when he was a young boy. "Butter your steak lightly using a bread knife and season with salt and pepper. Make your barbeque as hot as possible. Plump up your steak and place it onto the grill. A good quality steak should only be flipped once. The juices get trapped and seared into the meat from the heat, which increases the flavour. When the steak is cooked on the other side, it seals in the juices to create a tender and juicy meat." God, how he missed his mother's advice. Jeff felt the effects of his seventh beer as he flipped the inch and a quarter thick T-bone steaks over.

He pressed the steaks lightly with his tongs as he checked the firmness of the meat. He did this in order to tell how cooked the steaks were without cutting them. It was another tip he had received from his mom: if you took your index finger and thumb and made an okay sign with them, the fleshy part of your hand where your thumb was located would indicate the firmness of a rare steak. If you made an okay symbol using your pinky finger instead, it would indicate the firmness of a well-done steak. Each of the four fingers represented a firmness: rare, medium rare, medium and well done.

Michael had the table in the dining room set up with the well-used china set. If Jeff's mother's spirit was in the room, she should be pleased. The steaks and potatoes were served and the two men sat down to a meal fit for kings. Sure, the castle was small and void of any servants, but kings nonetheless. Michael cut into his steak and took a bite. "This is the best steak I've ever tasted. You are a magician with that grill." He grabbed a glass full of red wine to wash down the steak. He groaned and hammered his fist on the table with pleasure.

Jeff smiled across the table at his friend. His large bulk had always made Michael a very lovable guy, much like John Daly or John Candy except that Michael couldn't golf or act. He held up his wine glass in a salute to his friend of more than twenty years.

Jeff said, "To your health. May you never know the pain of a demolished soul." That somber note seemed to make Jeff's eyes tear up. He stared down at his plate of food and continued eating. God, he missed his wife and daughter.

Michael stared at his friend with concern on his face. "I can't imagine the pain you've been through. Did you call that number Mullen gave you? No person can go through what you've been through and not have some sort of emotional baggage. I think you should set up an appointment. As a friend all I can do is listen. Professionals can help you deal with your emotions." Michael continued eating his steak, which had seemingly lost its explosive taste due to the distressful conversation.

Jeff squeezed the water out of his eyes and replied, "I've got a meeting at the Geary Hospital tomorrow afternoon with a psychiatrist. Chief Mullen called ahead and told them my story. He's really made me feel good about my decision to come back home."

The phone rang and Michael jumped up to grab it. He nodded his head and came back to the table. "That was Jack. He says that he'll be over in an hour. I think you'll like him. He's just like one of the guys."

CHAPTER 82

MICHAEL AND JEFF sat in front of the big screen watching Kent State in March Madness. Kent State played a half to forget. However, that dismal first half seemed to wake up the team in the second half and they came on strong to romp Portland State 85-61. Once again Kent State would get no style points for their win. They played gritty in-your-face basketball, with 20 turnovers and plenty of desperation fouls. Thankfully they had two of the best backcourts in the NCAA, Jay Youngblood and DeAndre Haynes. Both players were good players who contribute in other areas. Jeff could never see such an undisciplined team winning the whole NCAA tournament. The team name, the Golden Flashes, seemed to be an omen to how the team performed: flashes of greatness. They should have been named the Golden Trojans or Golden Warriors. But, what was in a name?

Jeff stared at his empty beer mug and felt too drunk to make it to the fridge and back without incident. He tried the tested and true method and asked Michael, "Could you check to see how many beers are left in the fridge?"

Michael got up and checked, "Fourteen."

"Can you bring me one back?" Jeff smiled and laughed.

Michael got the joke and laughed too. "You know that I would've got you one. You didn't have to make me count."

Jeff laughed some more. "Yeah, I know, but this was funnier." It was good to laugh.

Jeff took a swig of his beer and the doorbell rang. Michael jumped up and opened the door to see Jack Armstrong standing behind the screen door holding a bottle of Canadian Club Whiskey and a phone book sized silver case. Michael opened the screen door and greeted their guest. "Come on in. It's good to see you didn't come empty handed."

Jack examined the room and saw Jeff on the couch. Jeff never turned his head to look at him. He just stared blankly at the big screen. He waved in Jeff's direction. "How are you doing? I'm Jack." Jack waited patiently for an answer.

Jeff finally looked over at Jack. "Let the dog and pony show begin," thought Jeff. Then Jeff noticed the bottle of CC. When his mother did drink, which wasn't often, she drank CC and Coke. He felt a chill ride up his spine and his stomach felt like it leapt into his rib cage and bounced once. He took a deep breath, raised his right arm, but said nothing.

Jack pointed to the bottle. "Since we're here for a reunion with you beloved mother, I figured her favourite drink was in order." Jack set the bottle on the side table.

Michael seemed awestruck by Jack's ability to walk into a room and know exactly what to say. He could see that with one sentence he had made Jeff a believer.

Michael spoke with enthusiasm. "Can I get you a beer?" His voice sounded like the small dog from a Disney cartoon; "sure Spike, anything you want Spike, can I open your drink for you Spike?" Jeff drunkenly looked at his friend. He could not hide his nervousness.

"Jack, tell him your story about meeting the biker in the movie theater." Michael pointed to Jeff.

Jack nodded and started into his well-rehearsed story. "Kinda funny story actually. I think Michael likes it so much because he is the master artist. Anyway, I went into a movie theatre and there was this biker there showing off his tattoos to a couple of girls. He was a big man and the crowds of people were listening to him and his friend brag about this skull tattoo he had on his shoulder and what the different symbols meant. Well, after ten minutes of listening to this blowhard trying to impress these girls, I'd had enough. So I stand up and look at the two guys. I was in the row in front of them and there were about fifty people behind them and I said to them, 'You want to see a real tattoo?' The ladies nodded yes." At this point Jack reenacted the scene and unbuttoned his shiny black shirt and turned around to expose his incredibly sculpted muscular body. On his back was the intricately detailed tattoo of a full sized Ouija board. "You could've heard a pin drop in that movie theatre. Several people gasped. Even the two tough bikers were speechless." Jack downed his entire beer in two gulps.

He stared hard at Jeff and said, "Ever since your buddy Michael put this tat on my back, I've been able to communicate with the other side. Your mother has been chattering loudly in my ear ever since I came in."

Chapter 83

Michael looked over to Jeff and saw that his face had drained of colour. He thought about all his good friend had been through and wondered if maybe the pressure of this meeting was too much to handle, even if he had a full liver of courage. "Jeff, are you okay? We don't have to do this today if you don't want to."

Jack seemed to take his cue. Somewhere in the back of his mind Cory screamed his impatience.

"Do it now! Right now! If you want to know the secret powers of the afterlife and have them at your control, you are going to do this right fucking now!" Jack walked over to an empty chair and sat down. He did his best to tune out the screaming in his brain.

Jack calmly replied to Michael and Jeff. "I've never seen a spirit with so much to say. If I leave here today, I can't guarantee your safety. Michael, you saw what it was like living here before you promised to bring Jeff home? Natalie has a lot of unfinished business to take care of before she can cross over to the other side." Jack folded his arms across his chest as he waited for their reply.

Jeff slowly rose to his feet; the colour had returned

to his face. "I'll need to take a piss first before we do anything."

Jeff stumbled over to the washroom and came back out several minutes later. He looked slightly better. He addressed Jack directly. "How do I know that you aren't just saying shit that isn't true? How do I know that the spirit I am addressing is really my mother?" He sat back down in the La-Z-Boy chair.

Jack pulled out the silver case and opened it. He pulled out the titanium Ouija tool with the clear glass eye in the middle, he put three shot glasses on each corner and filled them with CC. "First, a toast to your mother." Each man drank the whiskey. Jack handed the Ouija tool to Jeff and lit candles around the floor. "Place this on my back and your mother's spirit will answer any questions you have. This way you won't think that I am just leading you along."

Jack cleared the coffee table of the remote controls and magazines, took off his shirt, placed in on the back of the sofa and lay himself down. The rickety table made several sounds of protest, but held his weight.

Jeff stared into Michael's eyes. He examined the intricate tattoo on Jack's back and was truly amazed. When he closed his eyes, all the warnings he'd heard throughout his childhood about Ouija boards drummed a steady beat in his head. 'You can never be certain your friendly spirit isn't an evil one in disguise.' "You ready?" he asked Michael. The two men positioned themselves one on each side and knelt down next to Jack's back. Jeff placed the Ouija tool onto Jack's Ouija tattoo. He couldn't believe he was doing this. But, if his mother needed his help, he would do anything for her. She was the greatest woman he had ever known. Emily, his first fiancé and Sophia, his first wife, were the closest he'd come to women as beautiful on the inside as outside.

The two men placed their hands on the outside edge of the Ouija tool. Jeff asked the first question, "Are you Natalie Brooks?" The tool quickly moved to yes. Michael exchanged excited glances with Jeff, who wanted to believe he was about to communicate with his mother.

After they repositioned the tool to the starting point, Michael asked the next question, "Are you stuck between here and heaven?" Again, the tool quickly moved back to yes.

Jeff regretted all the alcohol in his system. His judgment seemed clouded and his mind overwhelmed. Everything seemed to be a dream. Still, he willed himself on and asked the next question. "What is causing you to remain here in this world?" The Ouija tool spelled out a name that sent shivers down the men's spines, C-O-R-Y-J-C-4, C-O-R-Y-J-C-4, C-O-R-Y-J-C-4. Cory Blake and the Junction City Four.

Suddenly, Jeff's sliver of hope for communication with his dead mother evaporated.

CHAPTER 84

ALL OF THE warnings about dabbling in the afterlife were coming true. Jeff watched as the Ouija tool slowly began to spin by itself on Jack's back. It was as if all the air had suddenly been sucked out of the room. Jeff and Michael were frozen in a real life nightmare. Jack's voice broke the silence.

It was deep and ominous. "Nobody moves and you'll be okay." The triangular Ouija tool suddenly stopped moving.

A very drunk Jeff and a very scared Michael retreated from Jack. Every ounce of Jeff told him to run drunkenly and bounce off of as much furniture and walls as it would take to get him to safety and never look back. He looked into Michael's face and wondered how he could still be sitting there so relaxed. Little did Jeff realize that Michael was gripped with an intense fear that grew with the knowledge that whatever happened would be his fault.

Suddenly, Jack laughed psychotically. It was a laugh Jeff recognized immediately. Jack's demonic voice spoke with a monster-truck announcer's excitement. "Did you really think I was just going to let you take everything away from me and let you go? Spend my money like it's all yours. Just who do you think you were partnered up with all those years? Your best and closest friend who provided you with everything you've got and are today. Jeff, do you hear me? Are you listening? Once we're together again, it will be like old times. Michael and you will be at my side and together!"

Jeff looked toward Michael who had the expression of a man who looked like he was trying to pass a bowling ball. He wondered how quickly they could summon a local priest to do an immediate exorcism. His drunken mind had difficulty understanding that he was speaking to Cory instead of his dead mother. Cory had crashed the party and taken over the host. Jeff shook his head that felt like it was full of cotton.

As Jack remained face down Cory's voice echoed in the room.

Cory spoke the terrifying words. "Don't shake your head at me. You think that you are in a position to disagree with me? Did you think I was just going to go away after you chopped me with an axe? You think you can leave me on a park bench to die? You need to know what it's like to spend your days struggling. I want you to pay."

Jeff had heard enough. It may have been the alcohol talking, but he did not care. "All I ever did with you was suffer. You killed everyone I loved. You're nothing but a parasite to me. Once I discovered that you were the cause of all my pain, you became a cancerous tumour to be cut out and thrown on the floor. I'd never sit next to you even if it meant all the . . . "

Jeff never had a chance to finish his last statement. All the candles in the living room had gone out. The dim oven light was the only source of light in the house.

CHAPTER 85

BEFORE JEFF AND Michael had an opportunity to jump back further from Jack, he had already reached down to the floor and picked up the titanium Ouija tool. With one hand he pulled on the bottom of the triangle and a six-inch titanium blade emerged. With lightning quick speed he lunged at Jeff and stabbed him high up in the shoulder area. The blade entered Jeff's body at the exact same location that Cory had stabbed him six years previous during the bank heist. Jack withdrew the blade and a castoff spray of blood covered the ceiling and wall.

Jeff felt the familiar pain as he crossed his arms in a defensive manner and curled himself to block the next strike of the blade. Jack shrieked like a wild animal in a rapid chant. "The Junction City Four must come back together. The Junction City Four must come back together." He stood in front of Jeff and aimed the blade for his next strike. For all intents and purposes, Jack Armstrong had become a brainwashed deranged lunatic.

The shotgun blast was deafening in the small living room area. Jeff looked up to see a fist-sized hole in Jack's chest as a fine red mist of blood floated to the ground.

Even with a serious knife wound his brain took in all the events in rapid succession. From his position on the ground his eyes scanned the streaks of his own blood on the ceiling and the blast of fresh blood that covered the living room windows and drapes. Oddly, what crossed his mind at that moment was how much of a hard job that was going to be to clean up; he would probably have to get new curtains.

Jack stared down at the hole in his chest in disbelief. He dropped down to his knees as blood gurgled from his mouth. Cory had assured him that it was going to be easy to kill the remaining members of the Junction City Four and reunite them. He gave him constant reassurance that Jeff was the threat between the two men, if he killed Jeff first, Michael would be a doe-eyed lamb waiting to be slaughtered. As the last synapses fired in his brain, he understood that the plan had gone horribly wrong. He looked in Jeff's direction as he fell face forward onto the floor.

Michael stood behind Jack as he fell. A light puff of smoke came out from the shotgun barrel. He looked at Jeff and asked, "How bad is it?"

Jeff laughed at the insanity of the situation. "I thought I told you no guns." He stopped laughing. He was about to bleed to death from a stab wound inflicted by a man possessed by his childhood friend. He listened to his body and started to feel nauseous from the lack of blood. He felt the sticky mess that came from the stab wound. The smell of blood brought back waves of pain. He'd never forget the emotional pain as he clutched Sophia and Emily while they were dying in his arms.

Panic began to set in. "It's bad. Oh, God! I'm going to die." Blood poured out from his armpit.

Michael quickly grabbed the phone and dialed 911. "911 what is your emergency?" Michael spoke quickly to the operator. "My friend has just been stabbed and needs an ambulance. Hurry please." The operator urged Michael to remain calm. Within seconds she had their names and address. She tried to get as much evidence onto the taped call as possible. "The ambulance is on its way. Tell Jeff to apply pressure to the wound. Who stabbed your friend Jeff, Michael?"

Michael took a deep breath feeling confident that he had done nothing wrong. "Jack Armstrong stabbed my friend and I shot him before he could stab him again." Michael could hear the wails of sirens in the distance as he pressed the blood soaked tea towel against Jeff's wound. Jeff had now lost consciousness. Soon there were strobes of red and blue lights flashing in the living room.

The operator continued, "Okay Michael. I need you to step outside to the waiting officers. Leave the gun inside and listen to their instructions. The quicker you do this, the faster the ambulance attendants can get to your friend."

When Michael stepped outside into the night air spotlights blinded him. He yelled to anyone who would listen, "Please hurry, my friend is bleeding to death in there!" Police officers placed him in handcuffs.

Before he knew it, an unconscious Jeff was rushed out of the house on an ambulance gurney. The attendants' spoke rapidly about Jeff's condition, "Patient is unconscious and has lost a lot of blood. A large amount of alcohol is increasing blood flow. Patient's system is in full cardiac arrest." The ambulance left with lights flashing as attendants feverishly worked on their patient.

Michael prayed and pleaded for his friend's life to no one in particular. None of this would have happened if only Jack Armstrong had not duped him. Shame and guilt of the situation washed over him. He buried his head in the wet spring grass and started to cry.

CHAPTER 86

JEFF HEARD A voice that sounded like a person shouting through a thousand-foot paper towel roll. He could hear his name but couldn't recognize the voice. The commands were very clear. Wake up now! Jeff forced his eyes to flutter open. The lids of his eyes felt like they had been weighed down. The room was eggshell white with off-white curtains. Although his vision was blurred, he was still able to identify the doctor by his white coat. Strange though, there were two doctors with identical features and movements. He was seeing double.

The doctor spoke to him in a very excited, yet concerned voice, "There you are. You are an incredibly lucky man. Welcome to the Geary hospital. There is a buzz amongst the Doctors here about your case. You see generally when a patient possesses a serious laceration to the artery, the window of survival is very small. In fact, it shrinks even smaller when the patient has consumed large amounts of alcohol because of the increased blood flow. What saved you was the previous scar tissue on your artery. Remarkably, the wound was not fatal because the previous stab wound created a ring of tough tissue." The doctor paused and pulled out a piece of rubber tube. He continued, "Imagine that your artery is like this elastic surgical tube. If I were to stretch it and cut it, the two ends would spring away. Now in the case of the human body, when they spring away, they get sucked under the skin and tissue. This means that the surgeon must go on a fishing expedition to retrieve them. You can imagine how difficult this becomes with all the blood. To put it simply, a little piece of scar tissue kept your artery from separating. You are one very lucky man." The doctor quickly left the room to continue his rounds.

Jeff looked over to his right and saw two blurry images of Chief Mullen come into focus. Jeff did not feel very lucky. He felt cheated. He had a serious case of the-"why me's?" And after all he had been through, rightly so. As he stared at the Chief, the image began to fix itself and the two Chiefs turned into one. Now all Jeff had to try and fix was his nausea. He asked, "Could I get some water please?" The Chief passed him a glass of water. The two men sat in silence. Finally, Jeff asked a question in a croaky voice, "Where is Michael?" He set his glass on the bedside table. The fresh stitches and staples pulled uncomfortably.

The Chief looked at Jeff and spoke. "He is being interviewed down at the station. It's a good thing you made it. Quite frankly, the story that Michael is telling us about the victim is hard to believe. If a judge were to hear his testimony about the events, he'd be facing jail time."

Jeff asked for his bed to be raised. "Thank you. Michael saved my life. Jack Armstrong turned into a knife-wielding maniac before our very eyes. We would both be dead right now, without a doubt in my mind, he deserves a medal for saving my life." Jeff repeated the same story as Michael. The Chief listened intently as he took down his notes. The Chief stood up and patted Jeff on his good arm.

As he rose from his chair he spoke, "This is looking like a justifiable homicide. We'll be confirming your story with forensics. As it stands now, Michael should be released and I'm sure he'll be by to visit you this afternoon." The Chief smiled, and then added, "I've always believed that some people are dealt an unfair hand in life. You've impressed me by your ability to play the cards you've been dealt. You'll be in my prayers." The Chief quietly left the room.

As Jeff floated in and out of sleep, he saw an older woman walk by his room in slow motion. He was unsure whether or not she had seen him. The sight of that woman suddenly made his blood run cold. The woman who had given birth to that demon Cory was only yards away. Jeff's monitor began to trill because of his elevated heart rate. His hands clutched the bed sheets in a cold sweat as Peggy Blake walked by unaware.

CHAPTER 87

JEFF STARED AT Michael in disbelief as he recounted the tale of his visit to the precinct. Michael waved his arms as he spoke, "I spent the night in the interview room telling the same story over and over again. Eventually word of your recovery got to the interview room and I started to dance around the room. That's when they figured I must have been telling the truth, as strange as the truth was. I'm so happy to hear you're going to be okay. When the ambulance drivers spoke about your condition, well, I thought you were a goner. Your colour looks a helluva lot better than when I saw you last. How is the pain?"

Jeff felt as if the pain in his shoulder paled in comparison to the pain inside his chest. It was as if someone had surgically removed small sections of each organ. Or maybe he had received paper cuts close to the nerves. The accumulation of all the past horrors brought him to this moment of his life. He stared into his friend's eyes and wondered if maybe he had lived long enough. "They've managed my pain nicely." The pain seemed to intensify with Cory's mother walking the halls.

Michael sat on the edge of Jeff's hospital bed. He looked at his friend with renewed concern. "Jeff I am so sorry. Are you sure you're all right? You know that I'll stay here all night with you if you need me to."

Jeff was awash with guilt. He reached into his drawer for his personal effects and pulled out his necklace with two keys. He passed it to Michael, pulled him closer and whispered in his ear, "Take these keys and listen to my instructions very carefully. The white van that is parked in the garage has a hidden compartment behind the bumper. These keys will open the metal panel and behind it you'll find almost four hundred thousand in cash. Pay the bills and take nice vacations whenever life seems to be too much for you to handle. Buy your parents something nice."

Michael wondered where this was all coming from. "Hey, I can't take this. This is your money. You spend it." Michael held the necklace with an outstretched arm like it was the plague.

Jeff pushed it back into his hand and squeezed Michael's wrist with all his might. "I'm not asking you to do this. I'm telling you. Consider it payback for what happened last night. Now I mean it. Get a cleaning crew to clean and repaint the living room. Throw out anything that has bloodstains. Please just do this for me." He released Michael's hand.

Michael had never seen his friend so serious. He tried to look behind his eyes to see if there might be more than Jeff was letting on. His friend had left him with no other choice but compliance. "You know I'd do anything for you. The place will look like new when you get back."

Jeff smiled and watched his friend leave the room. Several moments later he saw her pass by his door again. He grabbed his IV bag stand and stood up slowly. He winced in pain and soldiered on. Out in the hallway he observed Peggy Blake enter room 319.

CHAPTER 88

PAIN SHOT THROUGH Jeff's body with every feeble step he took. As he passed room 317, he bumped into a surgical tray used to remove stitches and staples. In another week or so, a similar tray would have been wheeled into his room to remove his stitches had he stayed there.

With steely determination Jeff turned to enter room 319. The shiny floor seemed to twinkle in the night time hospital twilight. He rested and gathered his energy. No one was visible from the doorway. Sweat beaded on his brow as he took another tentative step into the entrance. He mentally prepared himself for the accidental intrusion. "Sorry, wrong room," seemed like the right thing to say. He took two more steps into the room and saw the foot of the bed.

As he stepped past the point of no return, he turned to see Peggy Blake sitting quietly next to her husband, Fred Blake; her back was against the beige wall. Here was the man who had made it his mission to screw up his son's life so thoroughly that he became a psychotic serial killer. Cory's parents had turned their son into the killer who had murdered Jeff's fiancé, his mother, his close friend and two other people. The last thing Jeff had done before leaving Junction City for Mexico was to punch Fred Blake in the face. Jeff felt a new surge of energy come over him.

Jeff looked over at Peggy who looked like she had seen a ghost. Jeff leaned on his IV stand and pointed in Fred's direction. "What's with him?"

Peggy sat with her hands folded in her lap, her mouth slightly open. The years had not been kind to the wiry woman. Her hard life was apparent on her wrinkled face. She finally blurted out. "His liver is failing. He needs a transplant."

Jeff looked toward the old man asleep on the bed. Maybe there was justice in seeing the former alcoholic as he lay on the bed. He lowered his left hand where he held the scalpel he'd palmed from the surgical tray. "So he's in a lot of pain then?"

Peggy looked at Jeff suspiciously. She was never known to be a smart woman, but even a dumb animal can sense when it is in danger. "They've got him on a morphine drip." She pointed to the blue box that hung beneath the IV bag.

Jeff pulled out his little blue handled scalpel and showed it to Peggy. She screamed into her hand and fled from the room, she left her unconscious, beloved husband to fend for himself. Jeff looked down at Fred Blake as he stood over his bed and thought of how satisfying it would be to slice the man's main artery and watch him die slowly. He had seen it done so many times in the movies. As he stared at the scalpel in his hand he thought about what he would accomplish by killing Mr. Blake. Sometimes life seems to do a full circle. Jeff raised the scalpel with his good arm, fumbled around for Fred's arm and sliced off the morphine IV. The sound of the morphine as it trickled onto the floor was music to Jeff's ears. He wanted Fred to suffer for all the pain he and his demon son had caused him. Fred's face may have changed slightly to indicate pain: just like a baby though, it may have been gas. Jeff examined the blade in his hand and dropped it. Despite all the horrors he had seen and been through, he was not a killer.

Jeff stumbled out of the room and saw the nurses' rush past him in the hallway to attend to the beeping machines in room 319. He found a wheel chair and sat in it heavily. He was drained both, mentally and physically. Jeff saw the indicator sign that hung next to the nurses' station and wheeled his way in the direction of the arrow. He used his feet to shuffle himself along as he sat in his wheelchair. He chuckled to himself that he had an appointment today or maybe it was the day before. Maybe he'll have to pay a missed appointment fine. He wheeled his way up to the psychiatric unit-admitting counter and smiled to the pretty brunette behind the counter who had not yet seen him. Her nametag said 'Becky'. Jeff did not know how often patients, admitted to the hospital, wheeled themselves over to the mental ward. At this point in his life, it did not matter. He cleared his throat to announce his presence and said, "My name is Jeff Brooks and I'd like to be admitted."

- The End -